THE RICE-SPROUT SONG

THE RICE-

BY

A NOVEL OF

SPROUT SONG

EILEEN CHANG

MODERN CHINA

University of California Press
Berkeley   Los Angeles   London

University of California Press
Berkeley and Los Angeles, California

University of California Press, Ltd.
London, England

First California Paperback Printing 1998
Introduction © 1998 by David Der-wei Wang

The University of California Press gratefully acknowledges the support of Cyril Birch, Hsin-cheng Chuang, C. T. Hsia, Karen Kingsbury, Mrs. Stephen Soong, David Der-wei Wang, and P'ing Hsin-t'ao of Crown Publishing Company, Ltd., Taipei, Taiwan.

Library of Congress Cataloging-in-Publication Data

Chang, Ai-ling.
    The rice sprout song : a novel of modern China / Eileen Chang.
       p.   cm.
    ISBN 0-520-21437-4 (hardcover : alk. paper). —
    ISBN 0-520-21088-3 (pbk. : alk. paper)
    1. China—History—20th century—Fiction.   I. Title.
  PS3553.H27187R53   1998
  813'.54—dc21   97-37527
                                       CIP

1 2 3 4 5 6 7 8 9

To

RICHARD AND MARIE

FOREWORD

David Der-wei Wang

The Rice-Sprout Song (1955) is the first of three novels written in English in the 1950s and 1960s by Eileen Chang (1920–95), one of the most important Chinese writers of the twentieth-century.[1] Chang became prominent in modern Chinese literature in a roundabout way, since she spent most of her life trying to escape both the literary canon and the visibility of public life. When she turned up in Japanese-occupied Shanghai during the Second World War, she was at once welcomed and condemned as a writer of popular romances who was turning her back on the cause of national redemption. Her inquiries into human frailty and trivialities, her stylized depictions of Chinese mannerism, and her "celebrations" of historical contingency make her a perfect contrast to the discourse of mainstream literature, represented by Lu Xun, Mao Dun, and Ding Ling. But as the twentieth century comes to its end, Chang has proven to be far more observant than most of her peers in depicting China's tragicomic search for the modern.

Until recently Eileen Chang's name could hardly be found in any sanctioned literary history in the People's Republic of China; by contrast, since the 1960s she has been fervently embraced by Chinese readers in Taiwan and Hong Kong and overseas, thanks to the praise of C. T. Hsia and other critics. Chang became important across all Chinese communities in the 1990s, particularly upon her death in 1995. If one asks why Chang's works now appear more compelling than ever, the answer may be that as early as half a century ago, she was already practicing a premature fin-de-siècle poetics. Her words written in the mid-1940s resonate with a 1990s sensibility: "Our age plunges forward and is already well on its way to collapse, while a bigger catastrophe looms. The day will come when our culture, whether interpreted as vanity or as sublimation, will all be in the past. If 'desolate' is so common a word in my vocabulary, it is because [desolation] has always haunted my thoughts." [2]

To her critics and admirers alike Chang must have seemed utterly indifferent or even impatient. As if determined to live according to her own famous "aesthetics of desolation," she gradually retreated from publicity in the 1960s and became more and more silent and reclusive in her last few decades. After she was found dead in a barren Los Angeles studio on a fall day in 1995, her will disclosed a wish to have her body "cremated instantly, the ashes scattered in any desolate spot, over a fairly wide area, if on land." [3]

The Rice-Sprout Song came as a demarcation point in Eileen Chang's career. The novel represented both a new start after her relocation to Hong Kong in 1952 and her first attempt at writing English fiction. More important, it touched on subjects hitherto unnoticed in her works: the politics of writing and writing about politics. Among Chinese "Chang fans" the novel was never very popular, because Chang seemed to have dropped her familiar subject matter for something more epic. It also raised the eyebrows of those who insisted that great literature must transcend politics. But as will be argued below, *The Rice-Sprout Song* should be recognized as an important achievement, because Chang did not write the novel on behalf of any ideology. On the contrary, in the formulaic confines of the political novel, she manages to lay bare the constraints of propaganda literature, left and right, and to set up a play between them, in such a way that the volatile relations between politics and literature are fully exposed to view.

*

In the spring of 1952, Eileen Chang left Shanghai—her home for more than twenty years—for Hong Kong. Chang was not new to Hong Kong; she had been enrolled at Hong Kong University in the late 1930s, only to be forced to flee to Shanghai after the Japanese bombing of Pearl Harbor. The following decade, from 1943 to 1952, marked the most active period in Chang's career, ending with the Communist seizure of mainland China and subsequent control over all creative activity. Returning to Hong Kong in 1952, lonely and divorced, Chang had to make a living on her own. She stayed in Hong Kong three years, until in 1955 she embarked on the liner *President Cleveland* for the United States. Except for one trip to Taiwan and Hong Kong in the early 1960s, Chang spent the rest of her life in the United States. She never revisited China.

The two years right after her return to Shanghai—1943 to 1945—witnessed Chang's sudden rise to fame. With a series of short stories, she enjoyed overnight success in wartime Shanghai. Talent, however, was not the only reason for her popularity. She was equally known on other counts: as the last female descendant of an aristocratic family, as a celebrity noted for her shyness, as an eccentric paragon of daring new or archaic fashions, and as the wife of Hu Lancheng (1905–81), a flamboyant intellectual and collaborator under the Nanking puppet regime. At a time when nothing seemed to last, Chang surely found success in the brief moment of fame that was hers. As she remarked, self-deprecatingly, "seize the moment and become famous early; even if you make it later in life, it won't be so exhilarating."[4]

After the defeat of Japan, Chang's career suffered. Thanks to her noncommittal political posture and her marriage to Hu Lancheng, though it had ended by then, she was boycotted as a traitor by mainstream literary institutions. Eventually she took refuge on the margins of literary respectability, turning out clever scripts for stageplays and movies. But all this fame—or notoriety—came to an end when the Chinese Communist party established a new regime in 1949 and institutionalized the entire spectrum of culture in the name of the people.

Chang was never a productive writer. Between 1943 and 1947, she published two dozen or so short stories and novellas, together with a number of sketches, essays, and movie and art reviews. These writings range from accounts of decaying families to analyses of Chinese psychology, and from vignettes of life in Shanghai to exposés of social manners, demonstrating an extremely sophisticated mind at work. Partially because of her unhappy childhood in an old-fashioned family, Chang is at her best in gothic tales of moral aberration against the background of a stale society. Her total lack of confidence in human attachments led to another series of sketches and stories about romantic expenditure and romantic expediency. Whatever the subject, the notion of legitimacy, in literary, ethical, and romantic terms, is always at stake. Her best-known works are *Jinsuo ji* (1943, later translated as *The Golden Cangue*) and *Qingcheng zhilian* (*Love in a Fallen City*, 1943).

Ironically, Chang never thought she was competing in the league of highbrow writers. She drew her inspiration from popular romances and topical writings, and was content to settle among the "mandarin duck and butterfly" writers, a school known for its popular views on life and its fascination with urban trivia. In whatever she wrote, Shanghai was at the center. Chang was not a progressive writer by the standards of her day, but in retrospect, she has to be respected as one of the most sensitive chroniclers of China in a time of drastic change.

Chang enchants her readers above all by means of style. In sharp contrast to the high-strung, tendentious tonality of wartime Chinese literature, Chang's style is wrought with sarcastic rhetoric, witty imagery, and opulent symbolism; it brings to mind the ornateness of *The Dream of the Red Chamber*, the supreme model of the classic Chinese novel, as well as the mannered decadence of Western literature at the end of the nineteenth century. In many ways, this style is crucial to Chang's view of life. Under the unspeakable threat of Time, as Chang repeatedly tells us, one has nothing substantial or eternal to grasp. To survive, one learns to put up with the impermanent, and therefore inconsistent, *forms* of life. These forms, which find manifestation in signs, whether of language or fashion, are both splendid and desolate, both glorious and grotesque. Paradox is the most important figure in her writings and, to a great extent, in her philosophy of life.

Chang's popularity, then as now, was built largely on the works of this period. In the last three decades of her life, she published only a handful of criticism and fiction—much of it rewritings of earlier works—while she remained ever more secluded from the world. After the early 1970s, almost nobody was able to get access to her in person, let alone interview her. Chang's self-exile, however, aroused rather than thwarted her readers' desire; and they consumed anecdotes and hearsay about her life as eagerly as they did any of her works. One of them even obtained momentary celebrity by checking in at Chang's apartment-hotel and giving an insider's report—not on Chang, but on her garbage.

With the unwanted assistance of her public, an aura of mystery hovered about Chang, in a way not unlike that about her contemporary Greta Garbo. Then, in 1993, in a tell-all manner, Chang published an album of photos of herself and family members, followed by her complete works. From self-exile to self-exposure (though only in photos and words): Was this Chang's surprise gift to her fans? Or was it a last, desperate ploy to chase them away? Could the pictures resolve all the secretive images Chang had hitherto generated? Or were they enticing mysteries, more tantalizing to her readers than ever? Above all, through the eerie, elegiac sentiment evoked by the old pictures, chronologically presented and annotated, Chang seems to have arranged her own textual and pictorial spectacle of farewell to the world. Chang was a practitioner of classical realism in fiction, but in this album she may well have been an unwitting player in the postmodernist game.

C. T. Hsia, professor emeritus of Chinese literature at Columbia University, played a crucial role in enrolling Eileen Chang in the canon of modern Chinese literature. In his groundbreaking *History of Modern Chinese Fiction* (1961), Hsia devotes a lengthy chapter to Chang, celebrating her as the last major writer in the great tradition of twentieth-century Chinese fiction up to 1949. As he puts it,[5]

> Eileen Chang is not only the best and the most important writer in Chinese today; her short stories alone invite valid comparisons with, and in some respects claim superiority over, the work of serious modern women writers in English: Katherine Mansfield, Katherine Anne Porter, Eudora Welty, and Carson McCullers. *The Rice-Sprout Song* is already to be placed among the classics of Chinese fiction.

Before Hsia's rediscovery of Chang, a few critics of the 1940s had already noticed her; but none went as far as

Hsia in putting this woman, a writer of romances, next to such masters as Lu Xun, Lao She, and Zhang Tianyi. Hsia's polemical study remapped the course of modern Chinese fiction, and gave rise to an "Eileen Chang fever" in Taiwan and Hong Kong and overseas Chinese communities of the following decades. Since the 1980s, this "fever" has spread to China itself, as attested by the continued republication of Chang's works, and by readers' phenomenal response to the news of her death.

Hsia calls attention to Chang's capacity for moral scrutiny and compassion, a virtue that characterizes the best group of modern Chinese writers. But in contrast to most of her fellow writers, Chang's critique of social malaise never leads her to quick, ideological solutions, nor is her compassion reserved only for a select social class or activity. She understands the frailty of human beings before historical contingencies, and is willing to give equal sympathy to those who suffer and those who sin. This generosity nevertheless is derived not from her humanitarian posture but from her lack of confidence in humanity and her idiosyncratic notion of individualism. For her, individualism is a euphemism for self-interest and self-protection; selfish as it may seem to others, it is nonetheless the only way one can survive in a time of historical crises.

Some other traits distinguish Chang: her embrace of the material world, her aestheticization of eschatology, and her play with irony, which subverts anything hailed as solid, including her own writings. And she does not hesitate to generalize these traits and associate them with her vision of womanhood. Compared with the agenda of other feminist writers of her time, Chang's understanding of women's roles may sound rather passive, if not reactionary. She is nevertheless a most somber guardian of her own space as a woman and as a writer. She

knows well the importance of being not too earnest—
or not too politically correct, in contemporary terms—
whatever the cause. At a time when most Chinese writers,
women and men alike, were eager to exchange individual subjectivity for a collective, national one, Chang's
own brand of selfish and feminine mannerism stood out
as a genuinely defiant gesture. Little wonder that she
should have fled Shanghai, the ultimate spring of her inspiration, three years after the founding of the People's
Republic.

Eileen Chang stayed in Hong Kong from 1952 to 1955. To
make a living, she took advantage of her excellent training in English in earlier years and translated a series of
American masterpieces for the United States Information
Service, including Emerson's essays and Hemingway's
The Old Man and the Sea. But Chang's first love was creative writing. Under the sponsorship of the United States
Information Service she wrote two novels in English, *The
Rice-Sprout Song* and *Naked Earth*, and later rewrote
them in Chinese. Both novels have clear anti-Communist
themes and can easily be read as Western propaganda of
the Cold War period. In view of the fact that Chang had
been an apolitical writer, one may ask whether she did
not write in opposition to communism merely for eco-
nomic reasons. The problem is further compounded by
the fact that, when she left China, Chang had published
two novels, *Shiba chun* (Eighteen springs, 1949) and *Xiao
Ai* (Little Ai, 1951), both of which had pro-Communist
messages. Chang's movement from the leftist to the right-
ist camp in the short span of five years is certainly of significance. It bespeaks, however, not her opportunism but
her predicament as a Chinese writer trapped in the drastic imperatives of an ideological age.

As mentioned above, Chang is cynical about the myth of national salvation, a firm believer in individualism, and a connoisseur of fin-de-siècle aesthetics. During her three years living under the Communist regime, she witnessed the ever-tightening cultural control of Maoist policy, and sensed the rapid decline of her own creativity. Now in Hong Kong, she might be equally skeptical of the goals of the anti-Communist front, but felt nonetheless more compelled than ever to articulate her own politics. The result was a fascinating mixture of her recollection of life in new China and her reflection on the conditions of writing in an age of ideological warfare. *The Rice-Sprout Song* in fact *is* an anti-Communist novel, but it conveys the prescribed political message in a very personal way.

The Rice-Sprout Song portrays the horror and absurdity that the land-reform movement brought to a southern Chinese village in the early 1950s. The victorious revolution, followed by the redistribution of land, is supposed to liberate the peasants of the village. But contrary to their hopes, life does not turn around. Because of both natural and manmade disasters, the peasants are faced with yet another threat of famine, while China's involvement in the Korean War further deepens their misery. As they can no longer put up with the local cadres' pressure to produce grain, the peasants take to bloody rioting. The local People's Militia intervenes, massacring the rioters and further tightening control in the village. One last sees the survivors being forced to parade as part of the New Year celebrations.

Land reform was to be one of the most important policies of the Chinese Communist revolution in its early stages. At first glance, land reform appeared nothing more than a radical agricultural-economic policy. But the movement was never a mere attempt at revamping the rural infrastructure; rather it was always given a superstructural dimension, as its implementation contributed to, and was conditioned by, a program of drastic changes in traditional Chinese morality, legality, and psychology. As early as the mid-1940s, leftist writers such as Zhao Shuli, Zhou Libo, and Ding Ling were already writing about the triumphant consequences of the movement in northern China. Their works do not stop at describing the redistribution to the many of the land that used to belong to the few. For these writers, reform of the Chinese landscape will lead to the reform of the Chinese mindscape.

The Rice-Sprout Song rewrites the land-reform discourse proffered by leftist politicians and writers. As if parodying the jubilant undertone of Communist land-reform novels, in *The Rice-Sprout Song* Chang maintains a festive atmosphere. But as her story develops, this atmosphere turns out to be a celebration of something ghastly and theatrical, the prelude to a *danse macabre*. She details the chilling facts of food shortages in the newly liberated south, traditionally the richest agricultural area of China, and reveals the desperate moves peasants took to survive the impending famine. Her critique of Communist abuses, however, is accompanied by a deep sympathy with, and curiosity about, the human endeavor to undergo the test of life, however absurd. In her moral schemata, villains are detestable not because they are inhuman but because they are only too human. Hence the paradox that the most anti-Communist moment of *The Rice-Sprout Song* occurs when the two most disagreeable Communist figures win our sympathy rather than our hatred.

Upon its publication *The Rice-Sprout Song* was well received by critics in the United States. Major media such as the *New York Times*, the *New York Herald Tribune*, and the *Saturday Review* all reviewed the novel favorably. The *Yale Review* described it as a "good story that gives every evidence of being shrewd and honest reporting [about agricultural life in Communist China]" and opined that Chang did not "indulge in political harangue." *Time Magazine*, known in the 1950s for fastidious book reviews, highlighted the "mordant if melodramatic" style of *The Rice-Sprout Song* and concluded that it was "perhaps the most authentic novel so far of life under the Chinese Communists." For her debut as a writer of English fiction, Chang surely got enough attention. Critical acclaim, nevertheless, did not boost the sales of the novel; it disappeared from the market soon after its first printing, even though the publisher sold rights for twenty-three foreign translations and signed a television adaptation contract with NBC. Only years later did Chang see the teleplay of *The Rice-Sprout Song* in a rerun: in her words, it was "too disastrous to finish watching."[6]

After the modest success of *The Rice-Sprout Song*, Chang was commissioned to write another anti-Communist novel, *Naked Earth*, which turned out to be a disappointment both for readers and for Chang herself. In the fall of 1955, she left Hong Kong for the United States, in the hope of revitalizing her career. In 1956, she was awarded a grant to spend a year at the Edward MacDowell Colony, an artists' retreat in New Hampshire. It was during this time she met Ferdinand Reyher (1897–1967), a playwright and friend of Bertolt Brecht. She and Reyher fell in love and were married in August 1956. The following years were relatively more peaceful, in spite of the family's unstable income and Reyher's increasingly frail health. Reyher finally died in 1967. In the summer of 1969, Chang moved to the West Coast and became a researcher on Chinese communism at the Center for Chinese Studies of the University of California at Berkeley. She left in 1972 for Los Angeles, starting the last, solitary years of her life.

Hu Shi, one of the most important figures of the modern Chinese literary revolution, was among the first scholars to praise *The Rice-Sprout Song*. He sees hunger as the theme of the novel, and credits Chang for her verbal subtlety and emotive control, which are a far cry from the "tears and blood" style of propaganda literature, Communist or anti-Communist. Following Hu Shi, critics have all given credit to Chang's understated yet powerful narrative, but little has been said about the way she elaborates the politics of hunger. As a matter of fact, in view of the prevailing discourses of reform, Chang may have struck a devastating note by depicting the hunger that threatened the new China as a result of the reforms. The disproportionate growth of population in comparison with food supply has long been a peril besetting China's modernizations. When Mao launched the land-reform movement in the 1940s, he was aware of the fundamental problem of the Chinese agricultural economy and tried to tackle it with radical Communist measures. Together with land reform, "hungry revolution," it will be recalled, had been the slogan of one of the most enticing Communist campaigns in the 1930s and 1940s.

Chang's question is, If the hungry revolution has been successfully implemented why do the Chinese people still suffer from hunger? The leftist writer Mao Dun had published, in the early 1930s, the *Village Trilogy* ("Spring Silkworms," "Autumn Harvest," and "Winter Ruins"), through which he made famous a paradox of production: the harder the farmers work, the less they earn; the more grain they produce, the hungrier they are. By this paradox, Mao Dun intended to point to the irrationality of the prerevolutionary mode of agricultural production. *The Rice-Sprout Song* intimates that the same paradox applies

xviii

to the new mode of agricultural production. As Chang would have it, the old landlords may have been liquidated, but the communist government has become the single new landlord, with proportionately greater power and greed. The protagonists of the novel, Gold Root and his wife, Moon Scent, work hard to meet the increasing demands of the local cadres, only to realize that, however hard they work, they will never have enough to eat.

Beyond revealing the bitter physical consequences of the land-reform movement, Chang sheds light on the meaning of hunger at an ideological level. Whereas in an ordinary sense hunger represents a lack of physical resources—food, nutrition, and access to the normal circulation of foodstuffs—in Communist terms, it can mean something quite different. Under revolutionary circumstances, hunger drives one to the acute awareness of one's class status in the social hiearchy, thereby opening the way to radical solutions. On the other hand, in the same revolutionary circumstances, one's capacity to withstand hunger is a sign through which one demonstrates one's physical and moral strength. In other words, for those who are willing to suffer for the truth of history, hunger is not only the cause of revolutions, it is a mark of the true revolutionary, the outward demonstration of political virtue. If such an argument sounds familiar, it is because it strangely recapitulates the neo-Confucian (and Christian, and Buddhist) call for spiritual rectification at the cost of bodily deprivation. Early Chinese Communist literature abounds in works dealing with hunger, which testify to the writers' powers of realistic observation as much as to their willingness to suffer the consequences of exhibiting them. From bodily destitution to political institution, hunger as a spiritual state has been reified, so to speak, in the discourse of Chinese Communist revolution.

But in Mao's and his literary cohorts' hands, the motif

of hunger had taken an even more more superstructural turn. Instead of lack, hunger came to indicate its opposite, excess. Hunger is comparable to a libidinous drive—for revolution, and for communism—which always remains insatiable. It is easy to fill a body with physical food, but the spirit can never have enough ideological food. After the actual revolution, Mao is equally deft at playing the politics of hunger at the level of the imaginary. The unsolved but merely finite problem of physical satisfaction is replaced by the infinite problem of spiritual satisfaction. He constructs a mythology in which one's utopian desire cannot and should not be satisfied; hence the necessity of continued revolution. As early as 1940, Mao had made it a crucial part of his policy to feed his "people" with enough "cultural food." And in the following decades his literary followers would harvest endless crops of "cultural food" grown for mass consumption, on the pretext that in the cornucopia of Maoist discourse there is no limit to the hunger of the people.

It is at the juncture of how to cope with the threat of hunger that the two plots of *The Rice-Sprout Song* intersect. While Gold Root's and other peasants' families get more and more anxious about the forthcoming famine, Ku, a Communist playwright, is sent down to the village to collect material for a movie script about land reform. Ku's assignment is precisely to produce "cultural food" for the consumption of people like Gold Root and Moon Scent. But Ku soon finds himself with a writer's block, not only because he is struck by the difference between what he sees and what he is expected to write, but also because he doesn't have enough to eat. In desperation, he has to make secret trips to towns nearby so that he can get enough supplies. But the villagers are not so lucky; they are at pains to find anything to eat. Hunger has made them most inventive fighters for their lives.

Enter Moon Scent, the female protagonist of *The Rice-Sprout Song*. Before the land reform, Moon Scent had worked as maid in Shanghai, and was therefore more worldly than her husband and most other villagers. A pragmatic woman, Moon Scent understands that, to survive hunger, she has to store and ration food strictly, to the point that she even turns down her sister-in-law's requests. But despite her shrewdness, Moon Scent cannot prevent her husband, Gold Root, from rioting. After learning Gold Root has been killed by the cadres, she sets fire to the village barn, where she is driven by local soldiers and burns to death.

From Lu Xun's Xianglin's Wife ("New-Year Sacrifice") to Lu Ling's Guo Su'e (*Hungry Guo Su'e*), the hungry woman has become an archetype in modern Chinese literature. But more often than not, these hungry women are treated as passive sufferers, characterized by physical weakness and gender inferiority. They are walking symbols of a certain victimology, representing the suffering of Chinese humanity in general. Moon Scent is quite different from the stereotypical hungry woman. She is the most resourceful in her family; after her husband's death, she is not short of the courage to act upon her anger. But she is never a morally exemplary figure. She is a creditable woman only by Eileen Chang's definition of womanhood: selfish, earthy, material. It is Moon Scent who sees through the myth of cultural food and dares to transgress political guidelines in quest of her family's livelihood. Reading Moon Scent against other Communist figures in the novel, one wonders who is more sensitive to the material basis of life. Ironically enough, Moon Scent has to be killed, in the produce barn, to ensure Communist spiritual abundance.

Another significant aspect of Chang's fiction lies in her cool reflection on the conditions in which a Communist or anti-Communist writer composes history. Despite the sheer visible evidence in the village, Ku cleaves to the party line. He uses the villagers' riot against the land-reform movement as the model for a peasant riot against Nationalist landlords in his screenplay, seemingly unaware of the dangerous parallel he is inserting into his script. He is stunned *and* fascinated by the dazzling visual effect of the barn fire set by Moon Scent during the land-reform riots, so much so that he makes it the climax of his script, as a fire set by Nationalist spies.

The story of Ku may again illustrate the tension between the oppression of a totalitarian party and the creative freedom of a writer. But Eileen Chang gives this tension one more twist. Ku may have betrayed his political conscience by writing what he did not see and believe. But he nevertheless settles with his artistic conscience because, party line notwithstanding, he has organized words, images, and symbolism into a verbal and visual extravaganza *to his own satisfaction*. Is Ku's script a decadent testimonial to, or the tendentious propaganda of, a certain ideology? Has he acted out the cause of art for art's sake under a regime which depises it? Has he become a despicable accomplice in the collaboration of art with politics? And what is more in keeping with the principle of art for art's sake, after all, than the insatiable Maoist desire for ideological perfection?

In the afterword to the Chinese edition of the novel, Chang wryly tells us that *The Rice-Sprout Song* was inspired by a "reported" Communist cadre's confession about his failure to prevent a peasant riot during the land-reform movement, and by a Communist movie in which a barn fire was set by Nationalist spies. What she did was turn these pro-Communist materials against themselves. Not unlike her character, Eileen Chang has enacted, on the scene of writing, a cluster of self-reflexive ironies on the mutual implications of history and fiction, imagined truth and materialized myth. Her sarcasm about Ku's mission to rewrite history reverberates from her own work, throwing open the question of its intentions. Stranded in Hong Kong in the early 1950s, Chang was commissioned to write something she was supposedly not good at. She nevertheless managed to work out her own version of anti-Communist literature, a version with unexpected depths. Through Ku's story and her own afterword, Chang seems to have written an allegory about the vulnerable situation of Chinese writers of the time, Communist and anti-Communist alike. As the two regimes fought ferociously for the proprietary rights to history, Chang remained one of the few who saw through the gratuitousness of narrated history to a contingency of historical narration that would only become apparent much later.

To read *The Rice-Sprout Song* in an age when Taiwan and China are opening doors of commerce to one another and when Hong Kong has been returned to the vast embrace of its neighbor, one comes to appreciate more Chang's skepticism about political projects launched in the name of either historical necessity or revolutionary mandate. The final irony is perhaps that, forty years after the first publication of the novel, the hunger motif it so vividly portrayed has acquired a retrospective poignance. Recent studies by historians such as Jasper Becker have revealed that, between 1958 and 1962, at least thirty million Chinese people perished in perhaps the worst famine in Chinese history, one caused not by nature but by Mao's ideological vanity.[7] Little acknowledgment of this manmade disaster or its scope was made at the time, thanks partly to tight government censorship and partly to self-censoring China experts. When Chang wrote *The Rice-Sprout Song*, in the mid-1950s, she had neither the intention nor the resources to predict the forthcoming horrors, but in an uncanny way her novel foretold the cruel absurdities that would soon be imposed on the Chinese. A China watcher she was not, and yet she saw something inherently ominous by resorting to her material, commonsensical vision. "Our age plunges forward and is already well on its way to collapse, while a bigger catastrophe looms": a connoisseur of eschatologies, Chang made this mannered *and* sober prediction in regard to the China of the 1940s; with the publication of *The Rice-Sprout Song* this prediction proved all too true, and was fulfilled all too quickly, despite (or because of) all the official proclamations of an age of plenty. Where countless male historians failed to comprehend and analyze the condition of China, a woman writer of fiction managed—however reluctantly—to understand the nation and to narrate its destiny.

1. The other two novels are *Naked Earth* (1957) and *The Rouge of the North* (1967).
2. Eileen Chang, preface to the second edition of *Chuanqi* (Romance), in *Zhang Ailing Quanji* (Complete works of Eileen Chang), vol. 5 (Taipei: Huangguan chubanshe, 1996), p. 6
3. Eileen Chang's will, reprinted in *Huali yu cangliang: Zhang Ailing jinian wenji* (Splendor and desolation: A collection of essays in memory of Eileen Chang) (Taipei: Huangguan chubanshe, 1996), p. 53.
4. Eileen Chang, preface to the second edition of *Chuanqi*, p. 6.
5. C. T. Hsia, *A History of Modern Chinese Fiction* (New Haven: Yale University Press, 1961), p. 389.
6. Song Qi, "Siyu Zhang Ailing" (A private talk on Eileen Chang), in *Huali yu cangliang: Zhang Ailing jinian wenji*, p. 113.
7. Jasper Becker, *Hungry Ghosts* (New York: The Free Press, 1996).

IN THIS COUNTRY TOWN THE FIRST BUILDINGS 1
in sight were a string of exactly identical
thatched privies, about seven or eight of them. They had
a deserted air despite the occasional whiff of faint odor
in the wind. The afternoon sun shone palely on the
bleached thatch.

After the privies came the shops. And above the single
row of little white shops towered the dark bulk of the
hill, capped by two misty blue daubs that were distant
peaks.

On the other side of the pebble-paved street the ground
dropped away into a deep ravine. A stone parapet ran the
whole length of the road. A woman came out of one of

the shops with a red enamel basin full of dirty water, crossed the street, and dashed the waste over the parapet. The action was somehow shocking, like pouring slops off the end of the world.

Almost every shop was presided over by a thin, fierce-looking dark yellow woman with shoulder-length straight hair and a knitted cap of mauve wool pulled down square over the eyebrows, a big peacock-blue pompon sticking out at the left ear. It was difficult to tell where the fashion had originated. It bore a strong and disturbing resemblance to the headgear of highwaymen in Chinese operas. One shop sold sesame cakes and rock-hard black sesame candy rolls. Aside from these the counter offered two stacks of little packages wrapped noncommittally in plain white paper. A man came and bought a package. He opened it and started to eat right there. It contained five small sesame cakes. The other stack must be black sesame candy rolls—unless it was also sesame cakes.

Another shop displayed tidy stacks of coarse yellow toilet paper. In a glass showcase standing near the door there were tooth pastes and bags of tooth powder, all with colored photographs of Chinese film stars on them. The pictures of those charmers smiling brightly into the empty street somehow added to the feeling of desolation.

Hens stepped gingerly over the white cobblestones embedded in black dirt. And a man came down the street with a flat-pole on his shoulder, juggling a basket at each end, hawking more black sesame candy rolls.

There was the inevitable candle shop that also dealt in lanterns. Big bunches of little red candles hung down from the rafters like some strange fingerlike berries. The next shop was absolutely empty except for a little girl

2

seated at a table turning the handle of a bright green kerosene tin, turning out homemade cigarettes.

Sunlight lay across the street like an old yellow dog, barring the way. The sun had grown old here.

A passer-by, an old woman with bound feet, stopped the hawker to ask the price of the candy. Then she peered up at him and exclaimed with pleasure, "Why, if it isn't Lotus Born! How are your parents, and how is everybody? Is your fourth aunt keeping well?"

The man at first looked blank. But then it dawned on him that she was related to his fourth aunt and he remembered having seen her at his grandfather's funeral. She was a small woman with a short, concave face tanned a deep red, wrinkled and furling outward like a slice of sweet potato dried in the sun. For a hat she wore the old-fashioned black band that cut a pointed arch over the forehead. She always squinted as if the sun was shining into her eyes, and always talked at the top of her voice as if she was shouting across the length of a field.

"How do you happen to be in town today, Aunt?" asked the man.

"I came along with my niece here!" shouted the old woman. "She is marrying one of the Chous from Chou Village. They are going to register today at the District Public Office. The poor girl has lost both her parents; all she has is a brother. And with the sister-in-law gone to work in the city, there is nobody here except the brother. And you know the Chous are a big family and they are all going to turn up today. It will not look right if there are too few people on our side. So I have to come along."

She paused to squint up at him smilingly. "*Ai-yah*, what a coincidence—running into you like this. We have

3

just come and were resting our feet in the roadside pavilion. And I said to those two, I said, 'You people stay here while I go first and take a peep, to see if the Chous are already here. We do not want to arrive before them. It will not do for the bride to seem too eager."

"Is the groom here already?"

"He is here. I saw some Chous sitting on the doorstep of the District Public Office. I must go now and fetch the bride. It wouldn't do either to keep them waiting too long. And you must not stand here talking all day instead of attending to your business. Is business good? How much did you say the candy rolls are?"

This time the man refused to tell her the price. He picked up two pieces and thrust them into her hands. "Please take these, Aunt."

She pushed them away, looking offended. "No, no, you are being very unreasonable! Here I am seeing you for the first time in years. How can I take things from you just like that?"

"But this is nothing, Aunt."

"No, no! This is simply not done. Besides, I have no teeth and this candy is of no use to me."

"Take it home for the children."

"No, no, put it back there this minute."

The gluey candy, glistening black rods peppered with white, began to melt in his hands as it was pushed back and forth between the two of them. As his hands grew sticky, the man grew flushed and exasperated and found it increasingly difficult to keep smiling. He was only doing a duty, much against his will, and wanted to get it over with.

The candy finally changed hands. Vanquished by the

4

other's superior politeness, the old woman murmured her farewells with an aggrieved air and turned to go. The moment she turned away, the man's smile shifted ground —it vanished from his face to reappear on hers. He walked off with his flat-pole, his face set and strained, while she waddled along grinning happily to herself.

She went past the shops and the privies, out past the edge of town, toward the white-painted pavilion built for travelers along the road.

"Guess who I ran into!" she called out from afar. "You know my cousin who married into Peach Creek Village? I saw this candy seller and he turned out to be her nephew by marriage. I have not seen him for so many years, I almost dared not call out his name."

"Yes, but are *they* here? The Chous," her nephew Gold Root asked with some impatience. He was standing in the archway waiting for her. He was a tall young man, large-boned and good-looking, the color of dull, pale earth. His shoulders showed through his padded jacket, worn thin with age and faded to the lightest blue.

"They have come. I saw them. They have come."

"Then shall we go now?" Gold Root turned to his sister, Gold Flower, who was going to be the bride.

She did not seem to have heard him. She sat with her back to him, busy spitting on her handkerchief to wipe the hands of the little girl they brought along, Gold Root's daughter. The child was sulking because she did not see why they had to stay behind, and she had climbed up and down on the bench, reaching for the fan-shaped window, getting her hands all dirty. Later she was sure to smear the dust all over her aunt's new dress, a padded gown of dark red cotton print which

5

would also serve as the bridal gown at tomorrow's wedding.

Receiving no answer from his sister, Gold Root stood looking at her helplessly, his hands on his hips.

Big Aunt came puffing into the pavilion. "Why aren't you people coming?" she shouted.

"Come, let us go," Gold Root said to his sister. "Don't be old-fashioned."

"Who is being old-fashioned?" she said without turning around. "But you might at least ask Big Aunt to sit down and get her breath back. She must be tired—all this walking back and forth."

"Come on, come on!" urged Big Aunt. "Do not be shy. Nowadays it is not the fashion for maidens to be shy."

"Who is being shy?" Gold Flower stood up petulantly and led the way to town. With her childlike prettiness she looked much younger than her eighteen years. Her lips were slightly parted by a front tooth that protruded a little—not enough to spoil her face. Her hair was puffed up high in front, with a thin, long fringe low on her forehead that seemed to irritate her eyes so that she was constantly squinting, looking just a bit worried.

She headed the little procession, with the old woman dogging her steps as if afraid she might turn and flee any minute. Carrying his little girl in his arms, Gold Root trailed along behind them. Near the District Public Office the old woman instinctively moved closer and held Gold Flower by her elbow, guiding her steps as if the bride-to-be were blindfolded.

"Do not be feudal, **Big Aunt**. She can walk by herself," said Gold Root.

"Feudal, feudal," muttered Big Aunt. "I never heard such words like that until the new people came."

There was a stir among the watchers seated and squatting in front of the District Public Office. "They have come! The bride has come!" ran the murmur. Some of the Chous came forward, smiling, to greet Gold Root. And a shrewd-looking tall woman in her fifties, the groom's widowed mother, advanced upon Big Aunt and seized her by both hands. "*Ai-yah*, to make you walk such a long way!" The boy who was going to be the groom stood a little way off, smiling vaguely. Nobody looked directly at the bride, though she was by no means unobserved. She smiled a little, at nobody in particular, and looked around aimlessly.

After the greetings were over they all went inside. There was a whispered dispute as to who should approach the *kan pu*, or cadre, in charge of official affairs, and make known the nature of their business. The groom's side naturally should be given precedence and it happened that his mother was also the oldest of all parties concerned. But she insisted that it was a man's job and that Gold Root should go. Gold Root held his ground. In the end it was the groom's eldest brother who acted as spokesman. After stating their business they all crowded around the desk while the *kan pu* got out the right forms to be filled. Pushed to the forefront, the bride and groom stood before the desk with bent heads.

"What is your name?" the *kan pu* asked the young man.

"Plenty Own Chou."

"Where are you from?"

"Chou Village."

"Who do you wish to marry?"

7

He mumbled very fast, "Gold Flower T'an."

"Why do you want to marry her?"

"Because she can work."

Gold Flower went through the same routine. Asked "Why do you want to marry him?" she also murmured the standard reply, "Because he can work," as she had been coached. Any other answer would lead to further questionings and might cause trouble.

The bride and groom placed their thumbprints at the bottom of the forms and were pronounced legally married. But until they had celebrated the old-style marriage they were used to, the bride was to go home with her own family. Outside the government office the Chous and T'ans took leave of each other.

"Be sure to come early to dinner tomorrow, Big Aunt T'an," the groom's mother, said repeatedly.

"You go home early today and try to get some rest. You are going to be so busy tomorrow," said Big Aunt.

After leaving the Chous, the four T'ans walked slowly through the country town, taking in the sights. Gold Flower was very quiet, holding the little girl by the hand. They passed the only restaurant in town, a tall wooden structure which consisted of one big, high-ceilinged room entirely open in front. The unpainted wood was a streaky bright orange-yellow. In the semi-darkness of the interior dusty hams and big strips of fresh pork could be seen hanging down from the rafters, while crisp, cream-white sheets of bean-curd skin, long white cabbages, and the pale-yellow, bubble-studded masses that were dried fish maws all dangled above the heads of the diners. The cook was at his post in front of the white painted mud stove that stood right next to the door—the stove itself actually opened into the street. With a big

8

flourish he dumped noodles and other ingredients into the huge black pan. The mixture sizzled like pebbles in surf ebbing from a beach. And a young girl in postman-green pants was crouching in the street feeding firewood into the stove. The gaiety and excitement seemed to overflow onto the street.

The child stood at the door and refused to budge. When Gold Flower tried to drag her off, she wept and howled and, straining backward, almost sank onto the ground.

"Don't cry," said the old woman. "Tomorrow you will get nice things to eat. Tomorrow your aunt will be married and we will all be going to her wedding feast. We will eat pork; we will eat fish! But if you don't stop bawling we won't take you."

Even that failed to scare the little girl. It was a most embarrassing scene, with the cook looking on from inside the restaurant and the girl in green pants squatting before the stove turning to stare at them.

Gold Root bent down to scoop the child up, and carried her off kicking and struggling. He walked very fast out of the town. Beckon was shaking with violent sobs.

"Don't cry," he said softly. "Your ma is coming home, and she will bring you something good to eat. You remember Ma, don't you?"

Beckon's ma was working as an amah in Shanghai. But several months ago she had written Gold Root that she was going to give notice to her master and come back to work on the land. Gold Root was a landowner now after the Land Reform. But as they still needed the money she earned in the city, she had been putting it off. Now, no matter what Gold Root told the child, he

9

doubted if his wife would be home in time for the New Year.

They had named the child Ah Chao, or Beckon, short for Chao Ti, Beckon for Brother, in the hope that a boy would follow in her wake. But with her mother absent, for the past few years she had beckoned in vain.

"Don't cry, Beckon," Gold Root kept murmuring. "Ma will be home soon and she will bring you nice things to eat."

It did not seem to register. But that evening he overheard her asking Gold Flower, "Aunt, when is Ma coming home? Pa said Ma is coming soon."

He blushed furiously at being caught thinking of his wife, apparently yearning for her return. It was after supper when he was standing in the doorway smoking his long pipe with his back to the room.

Then he heard his sister's answer, "*Ai*, Ma is coming home. You will have Ma and you won't miss me." She sounded a little sad.

After he went to bed he saw that the light was still on in his sister's room.

"Better sleep early, Sister Gold Flower," he called out. "Tomorrow you have to walk another ten *li*."

"Aren't you asleep yet? Tomorrow you will have to walk double that distance. You have to come back."

The light burned on and he could hear her moving about her room. And he was filled with a sense of loss.

2

IN THE MORNING THE PEOPLE OF THE VILLAGE crowded around Gold Root's door to see the bride. Gold Flower sat in state while a chosen old woman combed her hair and made up her face. Actually, nowadays, with the hair worn short, there was not much to be done, and since Gold Flower had already applied powder and rouge liberally, the other woman merely made a few retouches. But it was a necessary ceremony, expressive of the wish that the bride would live as long and have as many sons and grandsons as the old woman called the *ch'uen fu t'ai t'ai* on this special occasion—the completely blessed lady. Big Aunt was disqualified because she had lost her only son during the war. He was taken away by the soldiers and had not been heard of since.

At the proper time the bride started out on foot for Chou Village, ten *li* away. A boy cousin walking in front of her beat a big gong to herald her coming. Behind her came Gold Root carrying Beckon in his arms and holding an unlit lantern—he wouldn't be coming back until late at night. He had his hands full so the bride carried her own bundle. Rotund in her thickly padded long gown, she had a big red artificial flower pinned on her breast, the same kind as was worn by Labor Heroes and newly enlisted men in the big meetings to recruit soldiers to go fight in Korea.

As the little procession moved through the village, the gong clanging methodically, everywhere women and children shrieked, "Come see the bride! Come see the bride!" A crowd saw them off at the end of the village. Big Aunt stood at the front shouting auspicious sayings. She would be going to the wedding feast later, with her husband.

"Where is that old man?" She looked over her shoulder. "He missed seeing the bride go off."

The old man was sitting on a small stone well topped by two boards, an open-air commode by the wayside. Sunning his back and smoking his long pipe, he nodded affably and smiled at the bridal procession as it filed past.

"Big Uncle, be sure to come early to the feast," Gold Root shouted to him.

"*Ai*, I am coming, I am coming," he called back. The old man looked almost girlish with his smooth-chinned, delicate oval face, his slight build, and the gathered fullness of the blue work skirt he wore over his padded

12

gown. His eyes were white and staring, half-blind from disease, and he had to tilt his head at a coquettish angle to see properly.

He and Big Aunt arrived at Chou Village before sundown. They took their grandchildren with them, leaving their daughter-in-law behind to look after the house. The wedding guests had already sat down to the feast. The bride and groom had the most honored places at the head of the center table, sitting side by side, each wearing a big red flower at the breast. A single beam of the setting sun crossed the room. The young bride looked like a clay figure painted pink and white, seated in the dusty path of the sun. There was about her an air of unreality and also, oddly, of permanence.

Gold Root being *shin ch'in*, new relative, sat at the exalted end of another table. Big Uncle and Big Aunt were led to a third table and after much polite arguing were coerced into occupying the places of honor. Four young women hovered around serving the dishes—presumably all daughters-in-law of the house. With prim dignity Big Uncle looked down into his bowl of rice, picking at it from time to time.

The food was very inferior for so important an occasion, but the groom's mother was a good hostess, bustling around all the guests, pointing out choice morsels, apologizing for this and that. She moved with surprising agility for an old lady with bound feet. Observing that the old man was eating nothing but rice, and very little of that, she fluttered to his side, a large, dark, slightly batlike butterfly.

"There is nothing much for you to eat—I blush for the poor food. But at least you must have enough rice—you cannot go home empty-bellied."

She snatched a dish of shredded pork and bamboo shoots off the table and emptied it into his rice bowl, all in one neat, well-rounded movement, catching him off guard. The old man was meek but there was also a limit to what he could take. He stood up indignantly. "How am I to eat this?" he demanded in a loud voice. "Why, I cannot even see the rice! How am I to eat this?"

But eventually he subsided and with a gentle, injured air started to dig for the rice buried under the juicy layer of pork and bamboo shoots.

The marriage feast was half through when the *kan pu* of Chou Village came in to join them. He was Comrade Fei, a serious-looking, round-faced young man with puffy cheeks and a fresh complexion. In imitation of veteran cadres like Comrade Wong over in Gold Root's home village he had let his padded uniform get very dirty to show he was too busy serving the people to attend to himself. A shiny patch of grease extended down his collar in a deep V. And like these old Party campaigners he had a face towel tucked at the back of his waistband, to wipe the sweat off his face, a habit which had been picked up from the Japanese soldiers during the war.

Gold Root had also adopted the style and tucked a towel under the string that held up his padded pants. Only the ends of white towel showed under his jacket at the back, but it was enough to make him feel a bit self-conscious. The towel had been sent him from Shanghai by his wife, and was quite new, for he never used it except for this purpose. Four red characters printed at the bottom said, "Wish you good morning."

All stood up to make room for Comrade Fei. After much ceremonious argument it was finally the old woman who moved over to have him sit next to her husband at the head of the table. There was no wine, but the unusual warmth of the crowded room in this cold weather and the effect of a full meal on empty stomachs made everybody look flushed and slightly tipsy.

Comrade Fei was friendly and convivial, asking all the guests how they fared during the harvest, how many *tan* of grain they reaped, how many catties of ramie. Gold Root had been made a Labor Model for his efforts during the harvest, and Big Aunt made much of the fact. She was at the top of her form. She had a word for everybody. To Comrade Fei she flung all sorts of remarks, which might not have direct bearing on the present conversation but which were always well-timed and musical. "*Ai*, everything is fine now! The poor have turned! Now things are different from before. If not for Chairman Mao we would never have this day! We will go on suffering, I don't know how long, if our comrades in Kêmingtang had not come!" Big Aunt mixed up Kunch'antang, Communists, with Kêmingtang, revolutionists, which only meant the early revolutionaries who had overthrown the Manchu dynasty, back when Big Aunt was a young girl. So she persisted in referring to the Communists as Kêmingtang and sometimes even as Kuomintang, the Nationalists who had been chased over to Formosa. But it was a pardonable mistake at her age, and on the whole she impressed Comrade Fei as being a remarkably progressive old woman.

She pressed the groom's mother to eat more, saying, "You are too busy looking after everybody else! You starve yourself!" And she said to Beckon, when the hostess piled food into her bowl, "See how this lady loves you! You stay here tonight, all right? Your aunt is staying, and you want to be with your aunt, don't you? Didn't you cry yesterday because she is leaving?"

The little girl went on quietly with her meal, her black eyes imperturbable.

Big Aunt tried to frighten her. "We are leaving without you. You are not going home with your pa. You think it is that easy—you fill your stomach and just wipe the oil off your mouth and walk off? You have been sold to this house!"

The others all laughed, and the hostess said, "*Ai,* you are staying here from now on. You are not going home."

The child said nothing. If she was beset by doubts and fears she showed no signs of it. But after dinner she went up to Gold Root and hung on to him, not letting him out of her sight.

It was after the feast that the real fun began, when the guests followed the newlyweds into the bridal chamber and thought up every means they could to embarrass the bride. In the old days it was a real carnival when most rules of propriety were relaxed, and uncles and grand uncles were at liberty to tease the young woman marrying into their family. "Within three days there is no difference between young and old," as the saying went. Usually on the next day, though, conditions reverted back to normal.

On this occasion people seemed reluctant to let themselves go, owing to the presence of the *kan pu.* But Comrade Fei apparently wanted everybody to have a good time and even took the lead in things. Gradually the guests warmed up and somebody shouted, "We want the bride and groom to hold hands." Big Aunt officiated as the bride's spokesman, making excuses and bargaining for her. After a lot of heated parley the guests won their point, but the bride and groom still made no move to comply with the request. It remained for Big Aunt to take hold of their hands and join them.

Then somebody demanded that the bride sit in the groom's lap and call him "elder brother." Everybody was convulsed at the very suggestion. The bridegroom made a desperate attempt to escape from the room but was grabbed hold of and pushed back to his seat on the edge of the bed, beside the bride. This time the negotiations took even longer.

"All right, all right," the man who did the most talking said huffily, "the bride does not give me face."

"Don't be angry, Uncle," said Big Aunt, addressing him as the bride would. "Let the bride pour you a cup of tea."

"Who wants tea?"

The bride remained adamant in her mute, unsmiling immobility. Matters remained at a deadlock until Comrade Fei suggested that she should sing for them as a compromise.

"*Hau-hau!* Good—good," the crowd shouted.

Big Aunt bargained it down to one song only. At last Gold Flower stood up by the table and turning to face the wall sang the marching song of the *pa lu*, the famous Eighth Route Army, which made its name stand in the popular mind for all soldiers in the Communist rank.

"Another one! Let's have another one!" Comrade Fei clapped and called out, and everybody took it up.

"All right, one more. But after this one, please let the bride have some rest. It is late now and perhaps it is about time for us all to start out for home."

The guests promised nothing, but finally the bride had to give in and this time she sang in her reedy little voice

"Hey la la," another recent song she had learned in Winter School.

> "HEY LA LA LA!
> HEY LA LA LA!
> RED CLOUDS IN THE SKY—*aah yah!*
> RED FLOWERS ON EARTH—*aah yah!*"

Comrade Fei came up and tugged at her arms. "Turn around and face the audience," he said.

When she jerked away he caught at her and suddenly started to laugh. His laughter was loud and clear and had a surprised ring. In the brief struggle she pushed him violently against the table, knocking off a teacup which broke to pieces on the ground.

"*Sui-sui p'ing-an!* Every year safe and sound," Big Aunt said immediately, almost automatically, punning on the word *sui*, which also meant "break."

Comrade Fei looked a bit uncertain, as if undecided on what attitude to take. Before his anger had time to crystallize, Big Aunt had already rattled on, "*Ai-yah.* Why is this bride so bad-tempered? It is all in fun! Don't you know that on your wedding day 'the more racket they make, the more prosperous you will grow'? Lucky for you Comrade Fei is not as childish as you are. If he takes you seriously, he might really get angry."

Then she turned to the mother-in-law. "Don't be angry, old sister. Our girl here has lost her parents early and has not learned any manners, as you can see. From now on it is your job to discipline her. But let it go this time—give me face. Please! Be as tolerant as Comrade Fei. See, he is not a bit angry."

Fei smiled thinly, straightening his cap. "This bride

certainly has a temper. The bridegroom better take care. Otherwise he is sure to end up henpecked." And he laughed.

The incident was closed but the mother-in-law's face now wore a very unpleasant look. The family had been put to shame in front of all the guests. Outwardly the bride was not to blame, but no doubt she had brought it all on herself. It was also to be feared that the *kan pu* might take it out on them sometime in the future. Of course the mother-in-law could not very well say anything, it being the bride's first day in the house. But the atmosphere was strained and the party broke up soon afterward.

Carrying Beckon in his arms, Gold Root went home with Big Uncle and Big Aunt and their grandchildren. The moon was out and they did not light their lanterns. When they had left Chou Village far behind and were walking across the silent fields Gold Root said grimly to the old man, "That Comrade Fei is no good."

The old man sighed. "There are always good ones and bad ones."

The old woman said pacifyingly, "He must be lonely. The *kan pu* never get to go home all the year round." Then she observed, "That mother-in-law of Gold Flower —she seems to be a capable woman. But I think maybe a little bad-tempered."

"That is no problem nowadays—there is the Women's Association," said Gold Root.

"Ah, yes, there is always the Women's Association. And now there is even talk of forming a Daughters-in-Law Association." A mother-in-law herself, Big Aunt smiled bitterly. "Not easy to be a mother-in-law nowadays!"

After reflection Gold Root said, "Of course it all depends on the *kan pu* in charge of the village."

The old couple said nothing to that. They all remembered the case of that woman in Peach Creek Village who had gone to complain of cruel treatment by her in-laws, asking for a divorce. She was tied up to a tree and beaten with a rod by the *kan pu*, who was old-fashioned enough not to take the New Marriage Law too seriously.

The people in the villages had previously been frightened by propaganda spread by the old government about the sharing of wives under Communist rule, the loose morals and easy divorces. So they were greatly reassured by the measures taken by this *kan pu* to uphold the old standards. Of course it was a most improper thing to do to ask for a divorce. But they did think her in-laws went too far when, after the *Kan pu* sent her back to their house, they strung her up and beat her in turn, breaking three stout sticks in the process. Breaking one stick would have been enough.

One of the little grandchildren cried out as he slipped and fell from the footpath. The old couple stopped to rub his leg for him, and Gold Root walked on ahead of them with Beckon, who had fallen asleep in his arms. The moon was high overhead, oblong, white, and cold, like a freshly peeled lotus seed, and the cloudless, colorless dark sky was a great desolation that closed down upon him all around. The crooked little path showed up palely in the darkness. Here and there by the side of the path, in the fields below, were the crouching forms of the tiny houses sheltering unburied coffins. Families who put off burying their dead because they could not afford the expense built those little makeshift houses no bigger than a man, complete with black-tiled roofs and white-painted walls. Too homely to be toylike, they stood guard in the fields like doghouses.

He had not gone half the distance when he had already worked off the dinner and was hungry again. At this stage it was not a disagreeable sensation, feeling all empty and clean inside and so light, almost as if he could easily walk upside down and romp around the moon. He wondered a little at this bottomless pit of a stomach which all his labors, year in and year out, could never fill.

Beckon suddenly spoke. "Aren't we home yet, Pa?"

"Shut your mouth—the wind is strong. Shut your mouth tight."

Heading for the darkness and silence that was home, he missed his wife more than ever. Just now at the Chous', the teasing of the bride had made him think about the same scene at his own wedding. The guests had made all the routine requests and had been more than usually wearisome in their demands, probably because his bride had been uncommonly good-looking. Even after they finally left, some of them had stayed behind to listen under the window and set off a string of firecrackers to scare the newlyweds.

People always said he had the most beautiful wife of them all. And maybe they would think that he had reason to worry, when she had been alone in the big city for so long. Women who went to work in the city often asked for divorces, buying their husbands off with a sum of money. Somehow he had never speculated on the chance of her doing this. Whether it was due to a great faith, or a great fear, or whatever it was, his thoughts had always stopped before they reached that point.

21

Perhaps he had been more uneasy than he realized, and had wondered about it too long, so that even her talk of coming home did not completely reassure him. Ever since she had gone away he had felt ashamed of himself. He had allowed such a small amount of money to stand between them. In sleepless nights he thought that she, too, must despise him in her heart, and it could never be the same again between them.

The thought of her burned restlessly in him like a precarious small flame cupped in his hands against the wind, its darting tongue searing his palms. He did not like to recall the last time he saw her. That had been the time when the soldiers were everywhere catching men and taking them to the front, and the country was not safe for young men. So he went to Shanghai to look for work, and to see his wife. He had never been out of the country before. It made him feel clumsy and gawky, the big city with its mountain-high buildings and roaring traffic, and everybody either snarling or sniggering at him. For the first time in his life he was conscious of his shaved head, his ill-fitting, too-tight clothes. He found a cousin to stay with who had a job as watchman in an alley. In the afternoons he would go to visit his wife Moon Scent at her employer's house. She would come down to the kitchen when she had time and sit with him on opposite sides of the greasy table, both facing front. She asked about everybody in the village and all their relatives in the neighboring country, and he made his answers with a half-smile, looking straight ahead, leaning forward with laced fingers and knees wide apart. The talk was desultory but they had to keep it up as there were always people around and it would look funny if they were to sit together without speaking. He wasn't much for talking; it seemed to him that he had never done such a lot of talking in all his life.

The cement-paved kitchen opened straight into the alley. It rained most of the time he was in Shanghai and Moon Scent would have his dripping umbrella opened out to dry with its handle stuck through the short wooden bars on the little door, painted a greasy-looking dark crimson. The orange oilcloth umbrella loomed big and bright as a setting sun in the dingy gloom. People kept coming into the kitchen and she would pause in their talk to smile at them sweetly and, as it would seem, apologetically. Often she would spring up to remove the umbrella from its perch, to allow them to pass.

For some reason everybody used the back door, the front door being permanently locked. Moon Scent said it was the same with every house in the alley. Bejeweled ladies going to parties in their shiny silk gowns and high-heeled gold shoes trotted past the grimy dark kitchen, and wet nurses with babies in their arms wandered in and out.

He frequently ate there. Sometimes when he came in too late for lunch she would fry some cold rice for him, pouring oil into the pan with a defiant air. She never told him about her mistress who now made it a daily practice to check up on their store of rice and coal briquettes, wondering out loud at the rate at which it went, hinting of a new leakage. Employers never liked it when amahs had relations who showed up in the kitchen. And in the case of husbands their displeasure bordered on disgust. Moon Scent still remembered when one of the amahs spent the night in a small hotel with her husband, causing no end of talk and shocked laughter in the household.

She never told Gold Root any of these things. Still, he could not help sensing that his presence embarrassed and inconvenienced her. At the end of a fortnight, when he failed to find work anywhere, he said he was going home. He went to buy the railway ticket with money she gave him. The trip had been entirely pointless, a sheer waste of her hard-earned money. He bought a pack of cigarettes for himself with the change, out of a kind of perversity which he did not attempt to justify.

Before leaving on the train he had called on her for the last time. They were expecting company for dinner and there would be duck-feet soup. Moon Scent was in the kitchen cleaning the evil-smelling bright orange webbed feet with an old toothbrush. He sat down and lit a cigarette, his bundle resting on the bench beside him. They had drained all their conversational resources during the past fortnight and there was absolutely nothing left to say. In the silence he heard something rustling alarmingly in the garbage pail underneath the sink.

"What was that?" he asked.

It was a doomed hen roosting there waiting for the cooking pot with its feet tied together.

The train was not due until hours later. Meanwhile, there was nothing to do but to sit there and wait until it was time to go. Moon Scent said all the expected things over and over again for the want of conversation, telling him to remember her to everybody. After she finished with the ducks' feet, she shelled beans. Then she found, to her extreme embarrassment, that she was throwing the beans on the ground and keeping all the pods. She bent down and picked up the beans hastily. Luckily there was nobody around, and Gold Root did not notice anything.

Having shelled the beans and plucked the roots off the vegetables, she swept the floor and threw all the rubbish into the pail under the sink. The hen clucked with apprehension.

When Gold Root got up to go she saw him to the door, wiping her hands on her apron and smiling absently. Opening his umbrella, he stepped onto the yellowish-gray cement pavement dimpling with rain. His heart was a trodden and squashed thing that stuck to the bottom of his soles. He wished he had never come to the city.

GOLD ROOT TOOK BECKON OUT FOR HER TO **3**
relieve herself before he put her to bed. Now
that Sister Gold Flower had married and left him alone
with the little girl, he had to take care of her himself.
He was not yet used to it.

Outside, the cold air was refreshingly astringent in
his nostrils. The hill overhead was a firm black bud
silhouetted against the pale blue-gray of the moon-
washed sky. Gold Root cradled Beckon in his arms, holding her away from his body with his hands under her
bent knees so that her fat little bottom hung down.
Nothing happened, so he said, "Sh—sh," encouragingly.
Actually Beckon was old enough to crouch on the ground

but he thought that the cold air was densest near the earth and was harmful.

The dogs were barking wildly. Lately he had always wondered if it was his wife coming home every time he heard the dogs bark. Still holding up the child, he turned his head toward the road. The orange blob of a lantern came swaying gently up the bend. The large red character on the lantern was of a familiar rectangular shape which he had learned to associate with the word "Chou." So it was somebody from Chou Village. It could not be his sister who had been home for a visit only a few days ago. And it was not likely that she would ever come at this hour.

It was a woman, though, who walked behind the bobbing lantern, and that was a big white bundle she had slung over her arm. When the lantern swayed toward her face, he saw something about her that made him whirl sharply around so that the child splashed warm urine all over his foot. In no time he had put her down and was racing down the road toward his wife.

He slowed down as soon as he came close enough to know for sure it was she. She smiled in recognition. And he called out, smiling, "At first I thought it was somebody from Chou Village."

"It was getting dark when I reached Chou Village, so I went to Sister's and borrowed their lantern," said Moon Scent.

"Oh, you went to their house? You saw Sister?"

"Yes. Her mother-in-law is too polite. She insisted that I have supper with them. *Ai-yah*, so embarrassing!"

He walked by her side. One of his socks, soaking wet, was now icy cold and tightly gripping the top of his foot.

He was grateful for the sensation because it proved that he was not dreaming.

"You saw Brother-in-Law?" he asked.

"He is not well. I did not go into his room because he was lying down."

"Not serious, is it? And how is Sister?"

"She is fine." She did not think it strange that he asked after his sister whom he saw so often instead of inquiring after her, when they had not seen each other for so long. She knew how it was.

"Is Beckon in bed?" she asked conversationally.

He turned and yelled, "Beckon! Beckon!" The child would not come. He had to go and drag her.

"Ai-yah! Grown so big!" Moon Scent laughed with embarrassment. She lowered the lantern to take a better look. Beckon twisted around to avoid the light but Moon Scent only held the lantern closer to her face. The child finally writhed out of her father's grasp and ran madly toward the safety of home. She crossed the courtyard blue-white with moonlight. The long bamboo poles the family used to weave baskets had been left out in front of the house. They made a great hollow clatter when she kicked against them as she passed. At this the dogs barked more fiercely than ever.

"Be careful not to trip in the dark," Moon Scent shouted, hurrying after her. Again the bamboo poles clattered under her blundering feet. They had inherited a room and a half in this old white house which was Gold Root's ancestral home. The rooms next to theirs were occupied by Big Uncle's family. And now Big Aunt called out shrilly from behind the window, *"Ai,* Gold Root! Is that Sister-in-Law Gold Root coming home?"

"It is I, Big Aunt!" answered Moon Scent. "How are you, Big Aunt? And how is Big Uncle?"

"*Hai-yah*, I was just talking about you. I said to the old man, 'What day is today? How is it—not back yet!'"

The oil lamp moved about behind the papered window and shadows shifted with it. The old man coughed and children woke up crying.

"Don't get up, Big Aunt, if you have already gone to bed," said Moon Scent. "I can come and pay my respects to you tomorrow morning. How is Sister-in-Law Gold Have Got?"

"I am fine, Sister-in-Law Gold Root," replied the daughter-in-law of the family.

"We are still up. And I was just talking about you," shrieked Big Aunt as she unbolted the door and waddled out on her bound feet. The old man also appeared, carrying his warming basket which held a few pieces of live charcoal buried under white ashes. It warmed the hands and feet very cheaply.

"*Ging-lai tzau!* Come in and sit down," urged Moon Scent.

So they all went into Gold Root's room. Sister-in-Law Gold Have Got also came. There were not enough seats for all but Big Aunt forced Moon Scent to sit beside her on the bed. "*Hay-yah*, Sister-in-Law Gold Root," she sighed, half-laughing, "I was saying all the time, 'Why so hardhearted—gone for three years and never returning even once!' Here the child is so big already!" She pulled Beckon, who was hiding behind the blue-and-white cotton bed curtains. With averted face the child clung desperately to the bedpost.

"Say Ma," prompted Big Aunt.

"Ma!" said Sister-in-Law Gold Have Got. "Say Ma, Beckon."

The old woman slapped the child on her behind and said accusingly, "See how big she has grown," as if she had done some mischief.

Gold Root stood awkwardly by himself in the shadows. The feeling returned to him that he had dreamed of this before, the scene of her homecoming, with those familiar faces crowded around in the dim yellow lamplight. Sometimes he seemed to be in it, sometimes not, as when he could not make himself heard amid the talk and laughter.

Big Uncle sat smiling and poking at the ashes in his warming basket with a pair of bamboo chopsticks. Primly gazing at a spot one foot above Moon Scent's head, he addressed a remark to her. "When did the rowboat arrive in town?"

"About noon."

After walking the forty *li* from town one should at least have a drink of water, thought Gold Root. He went to the stove. The fire was out but there was still some warm water left in the kettle, enough for a bowl. But returning with the bowl of water he stood confused before the roomful of people. He could not very well go up to his wife and offer her water, making her the sole object of his attention. With some awkwardness he went up to Big Uncle and handed him the bowl. Everybody laughed. Big Aunt snatched the bowl and passed it on to Moon Scent, forcing her to take it.

"See how attentive your Gold Root is!" she said.

They were all convulsed. Even Sister-in-Law Gold Have Got, who always looked unhappy, joined in the merriment. She had a long, bony face with straight slit eyes and she had a sad life. She had to do a lot of social smiling but her smiles always seemed dour and reluctant. And when she really opened up with heartfelt laughter, as she did now, somehow her face had a cynical look that was untrue and upsetting.

"They have always been a loving couple," Big Aunt guffawed. "All the time together—just like they were wearing one pair of pants. *Ai-yah,* it is a sin to keep them apart all these years."

"Look at this Big Aunt," complained Moon Scent. "I see her for the first time in years and she starts at once to talk nonsense."

"All right, all right—find me tiresome, eh? Let us go, old man; do not outstay our welcome. Let the two of them have a heart-to-heart talk."

"What have we got to talk about, an old couple like us, with the child so big already?" Moon Scent tussled with her to make her stay. But Big Aunt was coy. "Let us go, old man, do not make a nuisance of ourselves," she kept saying.

Laughing politely at the familiar joke, Gold Root helped to detain the guests, who finally let themselves be overpowered and pinned down to their seats. The teasing and joking went on. Almost like on his wedding night, when they made fun of the bride and groom, thought Gold Root. And his wife did look like a bride sitting on the bed, her head slightly bent under the parting of the bed curtains. Her beautiful eyes and eyebrows had a painted look and her face was a glowing silvery white, a bit broad at the base and low in the forehead. She made him think of some obscure goddess in a broken-down little temple. He remembered seeing an idol like that sitting daintily behind the tattered and begrimed yellow curtains in a neglected shrine. She was so beautiful that it was difficult for him to remember that she was his wife and at times he had beaten her when he got drunk or lost money gambling.

Moon Scent brought up the subject of the weather. She seemed anxious to talk about something else, thought Gold Root. Perhaps she did not want to be teased any more about him, he thought with a sudden pang.

"It has not snowed once this winter," remarked Moon Scent. "How is it in the country?"

"The rainfall this year was very good," said Big Aunt.

"Has it snowed yet?"

"According to the almanac the time has not yet come for snow."

"It won't be good if it snows after *li chuen*, the first day of spring. And *li chuen* comes early this year," said Moon Scent.

Big Uncle said querulously, after a short, uneasy silence. "It is bound to snow within a few days, my bones ache so."

Big Aunt said loudly, "Next year's crop is sure to be good; we have had plenty of rainfall."

"Far too much," thought Moon Scent, but she held her tongue. She could not understand the way they rushed to the defense of the weather as if it was their own son. She had been brought up in the tradition of pessimism. Whether it was out of fear of jealous gods or self-defense against the endless exploitation of landlords and governments and their agents, the country people never opened their mouths but to complain about the weather and crops, even among themselves. It had become second nature.

And now they were loudly praising this year's crops.

32

To her unaccustomed ears it sounded foolish and immodest, in shocking bad taste.

Big Aunt heaved a loud sigh and sang out, "*Ai-yah,* it is fine now in the country! The poor have turned! Old Heaven also helped—the harvest has never been so good! You have come back just a step too late, Sister-in-Law Gold Root, or you would have seen your Gold Root being made a Labor Model. Sitting on the platform, a big red flower on his chest—no son of our family has been honored like this! The comrade of the district government pinned on the flower with his own hands!"

Her practical nature would have kept Moon Scent from thinking much of such honors had they been bestowed on somebody else. As it was, she felt thrilled and proud. She glanced at Gold Root. He was being properly modest, pretending that his attention was wandering in a conversation which had grown tedious.

"It is not as if I am only praising him now," chanted Big Aunt. "I have always said to our old man, I said, 'To be frank with you, among all you T'ans, the only boy who shows promise is Gold Root.' "

Moon Scent said, smiling, "It is only Big Aunt who makes it sound so fine." She questioned them about the division of land. Then they told her how every piece of the landlord's furniture, all his clothes, all his household utensils had been numbered so everybody could draw lots for them. Big Uncle's family got a vase and a girl's silk gown, and Gold Root a big mirror.

"Where is the mirror?" Moon Scent looked around the room.

"It went with Sister's dowry," replied Gold Root.

"You had a fine mirror, a mirror of the highest quality, Sister-in-Law Gold Root—" began Big Aunt. But at the mention of that mirror, the usually timid Sister-in-Law Gold Have Got was so beyond herself with enthusiasm that she would not even let her mother-in-law finish a sentence.

"Ah, it was really elegant, Sister-in-Law Gold Root," she exclaimed. "Blackwood borders an inch wide, carved with a swastika design. It was easily two feet high——"

"More than that, much more," said Big Aunt.

"And with red and green streamers tied on to its corners on the day the dowry was sent over—beautiful!"

Poking his fire with chopsticks, the old man pointed them at Moon Scent. "You people drew the best of the lot."

"Yes, everybody said you were the luckiest," said Big Aunt.

Gold Root asked his wife, "Why, didn't you see it when you dropped in at Sister's just now?"

"I did not go into Sister's room because Brother-in-Law was ill in bed," Moon Scent said, smiling.

"Be sure to go and see it someday," urged Sister-in-Law Gold Have Got.

She had not even set eyes on it and Gold Root had already given it to his sister. Of course, if she had been consulted, she would never have said no, but she should have been consulted. She went on smiling but she was very displeased and felt less and less inclined to talk.

In time Big Aunt noticed her silence. "This time we are really going." She stood up, grinning. "If we stay on longer we'll be cursed behind our backs."

"What kind of talk is this, Big Aunt? Sit for a while longer," said Moon Scent, pulling at her arm.

"No, really! You must be tired. Go to bed early. *Ai-yah,*

at last the young couple is reunited. Not easy! Like those two stars that meet once a year across the Milky Way—the Cowherd and the Weaving Lady."

The guests filed out amid a fresh burst of laughter When all efforts to detain them had failed, the hosts saw them to the door. The light was burning low. Instead of adding more oil to the lamp, Gold Root took the stub of red candle out of the lantern, lit it, and stuck it on to a cracked blue-rimmed plate. It was an extravagance but he liked red candles for wedding nights.

When she had bolted the door, Moon Scent turned and said to him in a low voice, "I wanted to ask you all this time but I could not, in front of all those people. How is it that the harvest is so good and in Sister's house they were only eating *jho,* rice gruel?"

Gold Root did not say anything as he busied himself with the candle.

"The Chous seem to be so hard up," said Moon Scent. "We have been taken in by the matchmakers."

Gold Root laughed impatiently. "What do you mean—taken in by matchmakers! It is the same with every family. We've also been eating *jho.*"

Moon Scent was amazed. "But why? With the harvest so good we do not even have rice to eat?"

He jerked his head sharply toward the window. Without lifting his arm he motioned to her to be silent. But she went straight to the window before he could stop her and pushed it open. At that same instant the bamboo poles made a fearful clatter in the courtyard and all the dogs started barking, far and near. The moonlight had moved up the white wall, leaving the courtyard entirely in shadows. She leaned out and scanned the ground closely. There was nobody.

"Who was it?" she whispered after she shut the window.

He tried to sound casual. "There are always those loafers who have nothing to do and like to listen under other people's windows."

She knew people used to do that for an evening's entertainment. Life was dull in the village. But she looked at him and said, "Then what is there to be frightened of? What have I said that is wrong?"

He seemed harassed. "Talk about it later, will you? In bed."

She stared at him. Then she went slowly to unpack her bundle. She took out the pair of socks and pack of cigarettes which she had bought for him in Shanghai. Knowing him, she had on purpose chosen things which he could not give to his sister. For Gold Flower she brought a face towel and a piece of scented soap. These she had already presented to her when she passed Chou Village.

She brought almond shortcakes for Beckon, but she herself was hungry now from her long walk. She opened the oil-stained newspaper package.

"Beckon, you address me by name," she said to the little girl, "otherwise you won't get any."

The cakes were crumbly round slabs of an old-gold color. Beckon surveyed them with opaque black eyes.

"Call me Ma. Just once."

It was torture, but Beckon was powerless before the silence that walled her in and was growing greater and more insurmountable with the passage of every minute.

It ended with Moon Scent saying, "All right, all right, don't cry. You cry and I won't like you any more."

They both ate, and she passed one to Gold Root.

36

"You eat," he said.

"I brought them for you people."

"Save them for Beckon."

"You eat. There are plenty."

He took it very reluctantly and ate with great restraint. In the candlelight she saw that his hand that held the cake was trembling. There was a moment of absolute stillness in her mind, followed by a rush of anger and tenderness. What had the world done to him in her absence?

Beckon finished her cake. Nothing but a lingering fear of the stranger could have made her agree to leave the rest for tomorrow. As she undressed her daughter for bed, Moon Scent murmured, "*Ai-yah,* look at this padded jacket, so torn and not mended! Heavens, so dirty! And look at those buttons! Not a single good one!" Her mutterings were really directed against her husband's sister who was naturally in charge of such things during her absence. But the child took it personally. Tears welled up in her eyes and her quivering lips fell open.

"Crying again?" Moon Scent asked in surprise. "What is it now?" She pressed her face against Beckon's wet cheeks. "Hm? What is it? Tell Ma."

Beckon did not answer. Moon Scent lifted her onto the bed and removed her padded shoes. "Isn't it cold? Pop into the folded blanket—quick! Tell Ma why you are crying. Still thinking of those cakes? Then sleep early so you can get up early tomorrow and eat them."

Moon Scent sat on the edge of the bed, spreading Beckon's clothes on top of the blanket. Gold Root came and sat down beside her. He fingered the corner of her jacket where the slits were and felt the material. It was cotton with small mauve and gray checks and streaks of

37

red. He smiled slightly. It was difficult to tell whether he thought it too fancy or too expensive, or whether he was at all disapproving, though he seemed to be.

He warmed his hand under the skirt of her jacket. She squirmed. "I die of cold!"

"Cold? Go to bed then."

He leaned closer and she put up a hand and passed it slowly over his head. Her hand was rough; it rustled against the bristles on his shaved skull.

She whispered, "Everybody said it is good in the country, good in the country, good in the country. The cities are poor now and people cannot afford servants, but they do not allow employers to dismiss servants. So my employer was always telling me, 'It is good now in the country. If I were you I would go home and work on the land.' Now I realize I have been fooled."

She is sorry she came back, thought Gold Root. She just came home and here she regrets it already. Being together did not mean to her what it did to him. He spoke slowly, with a half-smile, "Yes, just now the times are difficult in the country. Otherwise, I would have asked you to come home long ago. I wonder if you can get used to it."

"Get used to it!" Her voice rose in sudden anger. "You think I had an easy life in the city?" She looked at him. Didn't he have any idea of what it was like in Shanghai?

He was silent. She could have said more but it was, after all, her first day home. She bent down and picked up one of Beckon's padded shoes and dusted it a little, turning it over and over in her hands, scrutinizing it in the candlelight.

"Did Sister make these?" she asked critically.

"No, her maternal grandmother made them for her."

38

"Oh." She thought with satisfaction, "No wonder. This doesn't look like his sister's work." Aloud she said, "My mother's eyesight is still not bad then, to be able to sew like this. I am going home tomorrow to see my mother."

"Better not overdo it—to go there and come back it would be another thirty *li*."

Beckon suddenly called out. "Pa, I also want to go."

"Aren't you asleep yet?" said Gold Root.

Moon Scent bent down to straighten her blanket and smell her cheek. "Go to sleep quick. If you don't behave I won't take you along."

But for a long time Beckon could not sleep, excited by the dynamic presence of the cakes in the room.

Moon Scent made her hands into fists and beat her aching knees lightly. "I suppose I am not used to walking long distances. All out of practice now."

He laughed happily, glad of an opportunity to scoff at her. "And you say you are going to your mother's tomorrow! I know you are no use."

She started to unbutton her jacket when she suddenly remembered to take the money out of her pocket and count it. He would have liked to know how much she had left, but she did not say anything and he did not want to ask. There could not be much since she sent money home every month regularly to help him out. Again he felt the prick of shame.

She took a long time counting, as if the sum did not come right. He did not like to watch her. He stood up abruptly and walked away to the trunks conventionally stacked at one side of the bed.

She looked up. "What are you opening the trunk for, at this hour?"

39

Silently he produced a large sheet of paper, smoothed it out on the table, and looked down at it, patiently waiting for her to finish with her money. Then he laid the land deeds before her and said, quietly smiling, "You look."

They were beautifully handwritten, marked with the biggest chops and seals. He knew the numerical characters and he pointed out to her where his name was. They pored over it, their heads bent close together in the pool of light.

She was very happy. He explained, "This is our land, our own land now. Right now things are bad because there is a war on. When the war is over it will be all right. The hard times will pass. And the land is always there."

Sitting thus with his arms holding her snugly under her padded jacket, it was easy for her to visualize the future that stretched out generations ahead like endless rice paddies in the sun, and one was possessed of infinite patience.

But she felt she had to make an effort to disengage his arms. "Beckon is not asleep yet," she said.

"She is asleep."

"Just now she was talking."

"She is asleep." Then he said, "You were not so afraid of her before."

"She was tiny then."

He was looking at a black spot on the back of her neck. Then he touched it. "I thought it was a bedbug," he said.

"There were many bedbugs on the rowboat."

"It is a mole. Hey, when did you get this mole?"

"How should I know? I have no eyes in the back."

"You never had it before."

"I could have grown one in three years, could I not?"

He laughed shyly. "Yes, it has been three years."

All that was left of the candle on the cracked plate were some drippings—waxy petals of a little red plum blossom. A long, thin flame came out of the heart of the flower and rose high and wavering in the air.

Beckon was dreaming of eating almond cakes at her grandmother's house. Her father and her Aunt Gold Flower were there, and many others. But her mother was as yet too much of a stranger to enter her dreams.

THE FROST ON THE TILED ROOF WAS MELTING 4 in the morning sun. A great dark chunk of hill hung above the roof of the house. Every tree on the hill-side stood out in the sunshine, with the trunk reduced to a thin white line, all but invisible, and only the light green foliage showing, so that each tree was like a flat green spot of duckweed floating over the shadowy depth of the hill.

Moon Scent looked up to the hilltop where little feather-duster trees stood black against the sky. The hill caved in a bit near the top. A little white cloud nestled there. Last night, in her long walk toward home, she saw a light up there and she wondered if it was a lamp or a star. If there was really a house up there, then this white cloud must be the smoke of cooking. It was certainly dissolving fast, she thought, faster than clouds usually did.

Last night, walking home in the dark, she had stepped on the droppings left by a stray dog. She wiped her cloth shoe with a wet rag and put it under the eaves to dry. The best thing would be to rub it with wine. She should go next door and borrow some. Big Uncle had always been fond of his cup.

But then, she thought, who would make rice into wine these days, when there was not enough to eat? She picked up her shoe and tackled it again with the wet rag.

If she had known what she'd found out during the previous day, she would have stayed on in Shanghai and tried to get Gold Root to join her out there. Of course it was very difficult getting a traveling permit to Shanghai. When she came back to the village, of course she had got her *lu t'iao*, road pass, almost immediately after she applied, because laborers were encouraged to return to the land. That was why one saw fewer pedicab drivers on the Shanghai streets, while ricksha coolies had almost entirely disappeared. However, if some people managed to hang on there in the city, she did not see why she and Gold Root could not.

If they both went back to Shanghai now, Beckon would have to stay with her grandmother for the time being. They would send some money back every month and her grandmother would be pleased with the arrangement. But Gold Root would never agree to go, not when he had just been given land. Once they left the village, they would lose their land.

And what if they could not find employment in the city? She might sit at a street corner mending nylon stockings. Perhaps she could borrow enough money from her former employer to purchase one of those kits containing the necessary tools. Nylons were still worn in Shanghai. They were either old stock or smuggled in. In summer, when nobody wore stockings, she and Gold Root could set up an open-air ironing stand, spraying water from their mouths onto the clothes they were pressing. She remembered that those stalls had done very good business last summer because they charged much less than the regular laundry shops, and nowadays everybody had to economize.

If all other schemes should fail, they would have to resort to picking cigarette butts from off the street to be made into new cigarettes, searching the garbage cans for marketable rubbish, lingering by bridges to help to push carts up over the hump, occasionally begging and even snatching foodstuffs from shoppers—which was not so serious an offense as snatching purses. They might persuade Gold Root's cousin, who worked as watchman, to let them set up a mat tent in his alley. It was a bearable existence so long as it was regarded as a temporary state. Any moment their luck might change.

Then she remembered what she had seen one day on the street. She had been walking to the market when she noticed that all heads were turned in one direction and people were whispering, "Look, look! They are rounding up the vagrants!" Two policemen holding a man by the arms were hustling him along to a truck parked by the roadside. The policemen were both smiling broadly and tolerantly, as if they were dealing with a naughty little brother. With his feet off the ground and his skinny shoulders pushed up high, their ragged captive was also smiling, a bit sheepishly. She watched him curiously,

44

knowing that he must know that he would be sent to one of the great work camps on the banks of the Huai River. There he would work on one of the new dams with great hordes of prisoners and conscripted laborers in water that reached up to the belly. She knew all about the Huai River; there were women living in her alley whose husbands were undergoing Reform through Labor.

However, here in her home village that was all very far away. She returned to the house and stood the mirror up on its stand, to comb her hair. She looked at her shiny black hair, cut to shoulder length and done up in a pompadour in front. This small oval mirror she brought back with her had long been cracked right across the center and was held together by a strand of greasy red wool. Ordinarily she did not mind it so much, but today, as she moved her face up and down to avoid that strand of wool, she could not help feeling bitter. Ever since she had come as a young bride into the house of T'an they had never possessed a single decent-looking thing. Now they had had a good mirror but Gold Root had given it away and she still had to go on using this cracked one.

"Sister-in-Law Gold Root," somebody called from outside. It was Sister-in-Law Gold Have Got peering in.

"*Ai*, Sister-in-Law Gold Have Got, come in and sit down."

"Where is Brother Gold Root?"

"Out in the hills cutting firewood."

Decorously, Sister-in-Law Gold Have Got stepped inside only when she heard that Gold Root was not at home.

"Combing your hair?" she said. "*Ai-yah*, what a pity you cracked your mirror." This reminded her of the other one, just as Moon Scent dreaded. Her faded eyes sparkled as she bent forward and whispered, "*Ai*, you must go to Chou Village someday and see your mirror. Really beautiful." Looking around cautiously, she dropped her voice further. "The fact is, if you ask me, you people could have kept it for yourselves. Nowadays who bothers about dowries when we cannot even fill our stomachs? Brides do not even ride in sedan chairs any more. They all walk to the wedding. Yes, ten miles or twenty miles, they all walk." She laughed. She had not been very fortunate in her life but at least on this point she could feel smug—she had been borne here in a flowered sedan chair. "Your Gold Flower also walked. That is why I say the times have changed. Why bother about dowries?"

Moon Scent smiled. She knew that Sister-in-Law Gold Have Got was a simple soul and was truly indignant on her behalf. Still, she resented it very much—as if people all felt that Gold Root was more partial to his sister than to his wife.

"Sister-in-Law Gold Have Got,"—she said the name affectionately—"indeed the times have changed. But you see when our Gold Flower goes over there she is not the only daughter-in-law. Those who came before her, every one of them had a dowry. If we sent her away without a dowry, we might be able to say the times have changed but others would think differently. Wouldn't that make things hard for her?"

Sister-in-Law Gold Have Got nodded rapidly but apparently did not take in what had been said. When Moon Scent finished speaking she leaned close and breathed into her ear, "Of course at the time, you understand, I had no right to speak, being an outsider. And you were not at home."

46

Thoroughly annoyed, Moon Scent spoke louder and with a sweeter smile, "It makes no difference, really, whether I was at home or not. I have always said to him, I said, 'You only have this one sister. Poor as we are, when Sister marries it has to look proper.' Unfortunately it happens just now when it is a difficult time for all, and we have nothing good to give her."

Sister-in-Law Gold Have Got felt slightly stunned and hurt. Nothing good to give her! One would think that the mirror was nothing of value, from this woman's way of talking.

Moon Scent asked her about this and that person in the village, and they gossiped a little. But the conversation soon languished. And yet Sister-in-Law Gold Have Got made no move to leave. Evidently she had something on her mind.

"The two old ones told me to come and ask you——" she began haltingly, her face reddening. "Since they are your elders they feel too embarrassed to open their mouths about this, but——"

They wanted to borrow money. They had a good harvest but a great part of it was gone after they delivered the Public Grain. There was only one tax nowadays, this tax called the *kung liang*, the Public Grain, but it was very heavy. And their silk cocoons and tea leaves had to be sold to the government at a riciulously low price.

"And we have been unlucky with our ramie," said Sister-in-Law Gold Have Got.

She told Moon Scent how the old man had taken the ramie to town to sell it to the co-operative store. He arrived early, when the *kan pu* in charge was still in bed. Annoyed at being disturbed, the *kan pu* drowsily stuck out a head from under the padded blanket to let the old man place a strand of ramie in his hand.

"Below grade," he pronounced at once.

The old man went home dejected. Then another villager, Li, told him that the *kan pu* didn't know what he was talking about and sometimes when the rejected ramie was sent there again it was accepted and even graded *tung wai yi*, first class above the normal grade.

So again the old man carried the ramie to town, in two big bundles dangling from his flat-pole. That day the co-operative was crowded with farmers, all bringing their ramie, and the *kan pu* were all extremely busy. One of them walked by and after a swift, sidelong glance at the old man's ramie gave it a kick and said impatiently, "Below grade. Take it away, take it away." And to make sure the old man would not bring it back again, they poured a bucket of red water over the white ramie. It was the new regulation.

The old man carried the stained, dripping ramie out of the co-operative and sat down with his load by the bridge. He sat there until nightfall and sighed loudly from time to time. Then he saw Gold Root coming out of the co-operative, a loaded flat-pole on his shoulder. Gold Root also had his ramie stained a bright red. His face was red, too. When he came over to the bridge, he threw his load angrily into the stream.

"What are you doing?" exclaimed the old man. "Not here, anyway. People will see you."

One of the *kan pu* had followed him outside and was yelling at him, "What do you think you are doing! Who are you trying to frame?"

"I threw it away because the stuff is useless now," shouted Gold Root. "I could have sold it to somebody

48

else if you don't want it. But who can I sell it to now, when you've stained it red?"

"I know what you're up to!" cried the *kan pu*. "You start a row and try to get the government to pay you, is that it? I know you people! And you there, old man." He turned and yelled at Big Uncle. "Why are you still here? You've been sitting here all day. Who are you trying to frame? Such scoundrels, all of you!"

When Moon Scent heard the story, she said, "Gold Root never told me about this."

"He was very angry at the time," said Sister-in-Law Gold Have Got.

Then she went on to tell about that time when everybody made army shoes for the troops—every family had to turn in fifty or eighty pairs. They worked at it day and night. Sister-in-Law Gold Have Got said her fingers bled from drawing the thick flaxen strings in and out of the *chien tsung ti*, the thousand-layer rag soles. They paid for a standard strong cloth for the uppers and for a flimsier kind for the lining. Everything cost money, even the flaxen strings and the rags bought by the catty, to make the soles out of.

The *kan pu* visisted each family in turn, spurring them on where the work lagged, and where it was coming along nicely, talking them into another twenty pairs. "Make the soles thick and strong," he urged. "Our warriors will go far in those shoes, thousands of *li* away, to Korea, where they are fighting the American devils. If we don't drive the American imperialists back from the Yalu River, they'll be here at our door. And the first thing, your land will be taken away from you."

"Stupid!" Big Aunt had murmured when the *kan pu* was gone. "The American devils will never come to this

49

little village. Besides, these *kan pu* have left us so poor that there's nothing for the foreign devils to steal anyway!"

When the shoes were made, there was the Support-Frontlines Contribution; always one thing after another. But the worst was the Contribute-Airplanes-and-Big-Guns Movement, when Chou Village was forced to "challenge" this village. Sister-in-Law Gold Have Got could not get the new terms straight but she gave a much clearer account than Gold Root had given last night. Gold Root was fumbling and evasive throughout, not because he did not want to tell her but because he was all mixed up in his own mind.

"Sister-in-Law Gold Root, what I told you you must not repeat to Brother Gold Root," cautioned Sister-in-Law Gold Have Got. "Not even to our two old ones. If they know I told you all this they would be frightened to death."

Moon Scent knew that they were afraid of Gold Root because he was a Labor Model. "If I had known it was like this in the country, I would never have come back," she sighed. It was her turn to tell of her woes. "You know how things are with us, Sister-in-Law Gold Have Got. The whole family depended on what little I earned in the city. And there I had to take care of my own clothes, shoes, socks, and bedding. And things are so expensive in Shanghai. How could I have any money saved up?"

"Better than us, anyhow." Again Sister-in-Law Gold Have Got brought her face close to Moon Scent's and whispered. "People used to say, 'The poor depend on the rich, the rich depend on Heaven.' At least in the old days when there was a famine we could go to the landlord to borrow some rice." Then she heard the folding doors creak in the courtyard and darted out to look.

It was Gold Root coming back with the firewood. He shouldered a flat-pole hung with two enormous bundles of leafy branches which, sticking out in all directions, came to the height of a man and a half. He looked as if he had a giant, untidy bird perched on his shoulders with shaggy wings outstretched. After several attempts he managed to edge in sideways through the door.

At his return Sister-in-Law Gold Have Got disappeared. But all through the morning the people of the village came to greet Moon Scent at her house and every one of them tried to borrow money. They asked for very little, and they came without hope and left without rancor.

Moon Scent grew frightened. She told Gold Root, "You would think that I've returned after making a fortune, the way everybody comes to me for money."

"It has always been like this," he said, smiling and on the defensive as usual. "Anyone who comes back from the city, everybody always thinks he's made a fortune."

He wanted her to wash sufficient rice for them to have a meal of properly cooked rice for lunch.

"No, we really shouldn't," said Moon Scent. "There is so little left as it is. It won't last us through spring if we don't watch out."

"It's only once in a while."

"But why today of all days? It's neither the New Year nor a festival, and your birthday is past now," she said, half-laughing. She wanted to hear him say right out that this was her first day home and called for celebration.

But he merely looked embarrassed and said stubbornly,

"No reason. I haven't had solid rice for a long time, and I feel like having some."

At last she gave in. But when she bent low into the great earthen jar to dip for rice, her hand faltered. She compromised by cooking a pot of thick rice gruel.

Before they sat down to lunch Gold Root went to close the door. "If people see us eating like this they would have more reason for coming to borrow money."

"Close the door in broad daylight!" she exclaimed. "What would people think? They would die laughing!" Doors were never closed except at bedtime, no matter how cold the weather.

So Gold Root ate standing up near the open door, listening to every sound outside. He suddenly grew tense. "Clear it away quick," he whispered, "Comrade Wong is coming!"

Already somebody was calling heartily from outside in the unfamiliar accent of another dialect, "Is Gold Root there?"

Thrusting his bowl into Moon Scent's hands, Gold Root hurried out into the courtyard. Moon Scent put both their bowls on the bed against the pillow, where the bed curtains hid them from view. It being rice gruel, however thick, she had to be careful not to upset the bowl and spill it. Then she turned to Beckon to snatch the bowl from her hand. But Beckon refused to let go and Moon Scent was afraid that the sticky gruel, scalding hot, would spill on the child's hands. By this time Gold Root had already walked in with Comrade Wong.

Wong was a small man over forty but his lean face still looked young under his cap and he had an attractive smile. His thickly wadded uniform made him look much stouter than he was, and with a tight waistband it gave him a bosom and a bustle.

"Well, is this Sister-in-Law Gold Root?" he said pleasantly. "You people go on with your meal. Go on. Please. I have come at an inopportune moment."

They insisted that they had finished eating, and Beckon timidly set her bowl down on the chair. Wong grinned at her. "Finish your gruel before it gets cold, Beckon. Grown taller again." He held her up high above his head. Beckon continued to look glum though secretly she was thrilled.

"Please sit down, Comrade Wong," Moon Scent said, smiling. Rushing to the stove, she poured him a bowl of hot water. "No tea leaves even. Drink a bowl of water, Comrade Wong."

"Don't bother, Sister-in-Law Gold Root. Don't make me feel like I'm an outsider." Wong raised himself slightly in his chair in acknowledgment of the hot water. "Just came back last night? Must be tired after the journey."

Moon Scent showed him her "road chit."

"*Hau, hau!* Good, good," said Wong as he read it. "Good, good! 'Return to the Country to Produce'—very good." He drew up one leg and placed his foot on the bench, peasant fashion. "Sister-in-Law Gold Root, this time you came back you must have noticed that the country is different from before. You know the poor have stood up. Now the government is the people's own government. All your own people. Any opinion you have, you can tell it to us. Now don't be afraid—you know the people have turned over!"

Then he praised Gold Root and said, "Now you have come back—very good. The two of you would co-operate in Handling Production. With production boosted up you would also Study Culture. Right now in winter, when there is not much work to be done, everybody goes to Winter School. We have Little Teachers who come here from the school in town to teach us. Sister-in-Law Gold Root, nowadays men and women are all the same; you two should compete with each other. Since he is a Labor Model you should be a Study Model." They all laughed together.

After a while Comrade Wong rose and left. Gold Root and Moon Scent saw him out of the courtyard. When they returned she said, "This Comrade Wong is really good. He did not even touch the water. Not like those officers in the old days, always wanting this and that. Once they stepped inside the door, they wouldn't be satisfied unless you killed a chicken for their dinner."

No stranger had ever spoken to her like that before, so pleasantly, taking such an earnest interest in her, and as a person instead of as a woman. She was very impressed.

"Comrade Wong is a good man," said Gold Root.

But she noticed that he was miserable all day because that bowl of thick rice gruel had been seen by Wong.

She explained to him that Beckon had held on to it and when she had tried to wrench it away she was nervous about spilling the hot gruel on the child's hand. Then she lost her temper and said, "It is all your fault. You insisted on putting in more rice."

"If you really listened to me and cooked solid rice, it would have been all right—solid rice won't spill."

"All right, blame it on me." And she muttered, "It is you who want to eat. And it is you who are afraid."

"I want to eat solid rice, not this sticky mush."

54

"Don't eat it then. Who's forcing you?"

She slapped the cold gruel back to the pot and warmed it. He finished his portion in silence.

After lunch she went down to the stream to do some washing. Squatting at the bottom of the stone steps, she lifted her club and pounded the clothes. Suddenly the hills on the opposite bank boomed out the sound of a colossal drum. She remembered how startled she was when she first married into this village and came to wash clothes by the stream for the first time. It was incredible to think that this slow "Boom! Boom!" was only an echo of her pounding clothes. She always felt that something of great moment was happening on the other bank, high up in the hills, in the depth of the woods. It was as if the ancient gods were at war.

Two geese floated nearby in the stream. Their apricot-yellow legs trailed behind them like ribbons in the pale green water.

"Ma! Grandmother has come!" Beckon came running, shouting from afar.

She was planning to visit her mother tomorrow but apparently her mother had already heard of her return and could not wait to see her. On the rowboat she had met two men from her native village. They must have told her mother.

She wrung her clothes dry and hurried home with Beckon.

Gold Root was sitting with her mother, keeping her company. Moon Scent had never been a favorite with her mother. But not having seen each other for some years, they both felt a little sad when they met. Her mother had aged. They talked about the births, deaths, and marriages in the family and among relatives. Her mother spoke of a cousin who died of "the sickness of vomiting blood." It turned out that he had become ill from being strung up by the heels and beaten with a stick by the village cadres. She got well started on the story before she checked herself. Then she sighed and merely said, "Your Comrade Wong is good."

After a while Gold Root went out into the courtyard and stood at the gate smoking his long pipe, to leave them alone together, as it was always assumed that a mother and daughter would have very private things to say to each other. He was sure her mother would want to borrow money from her. They were inside for a long time.

When her mother left they walked her to the mouth of the village. In this hilly country the temperature dropped sharply the moment the sun went down. A cold wind breathed forth from the gray-green bamboo forest. Husband and wife stood holding Beckon by the hand, watching the old woman disappear down the road. Gold Root guessed that Moon Scent must have lent her mother all her money and she was not happy about it.

LESS THAN A WEEK AFTER SHE HAD WALKED **5** up the path to greet her husband, Moon Scent already felt completely settled down, as if she had never been away.

In the morning Gold Root worked in the courtyard, splitting bamboos into halves, then slicing them thin. After this he rested for a while. He dragged out two huge baskets from indoors, fetched a chair, and sat down facing the baskets, smoking his long pipe. They were handsome to look at, made with split bamboos woven into a pattern of big white and pale green squares.

Then, squatting on the ground, he passed the long slices of bamboo through the basket to make a handle.

He grew hot from working so he removed his padded jacket and piled it on the chair.

A younger cousin returning from the hills carried on his shoulder a bundle of quivering long bamboos eight or nine yards in length. Coming into the courtyard, he shed the bamboos on the ground with a tremendous crash. Gold Root did not even look up.

Moon Scent came out and sat under the eaves mending the jacket Gold Root had taken off. They both sat facing the sun, Gold Root more out in front. The sun sailed slowly into the clouds and emerged as slowly. The earth brightened and dulled many times. But the husband and wife never once spoke to each other.

With the warmth of the sun upon her, Moon Scent felt itchy at the waist. She lifted her jacket, revealing a good deal of yellowish pale flesh. She scratched the skin into a dull red flush, then, inspired by a sudden suspicion, seized Gold Root's jacket. She spread it out and looked it over carefully. Nothing there. Then, turning one sleeve inside out, she went on with her mending.

When Gold Root finished the handle of a basket, he would set one foot inside and try to lift it by the handle. The handle remained firm. Big Uncle hurried by with his hands inside his sleeves, but seeing the new basket he stopped to set one foot inside and try the strength of the handle, too. Finding it satisfactory, he walked away without a word. Other kinsmen crossed the courtyard. Every one of them paused to step on the basket and try the handle, only to pass on without comment.

Moon Scent brought out bowls and chopsticks and set them on the table in the open. In the middle of the table she placed a bowl of blackish cubes of salted vegetables, and on one side a tall wooden bucket holding the rice gruel. Beckon had appeared from nowhere to hang around the table.

"Hey, come have your lunch," Gold Root called out gaily to the child, quite unnecessarily, since his daughter had already fetched her own stool. The first time he picked up some vegetable with his chopsticks he deposited it in her bowl.

Moon Scent scarcely touched the vegetable. It was unseemly for a woman to be too interested in tasty things. But when Gold Root turned to refill his bowl she quickly took some of it, twice.

A yellow dog looking for nonexistent scraps under the table burrowed under Gold Root's chair. The fluffy tail waved at Gold Root's rear exactly as if it were Gold Root's tail.

Big Aunt passed by. She craned her neck to have a good look at what they were eating. Then she walked on without saying anything. Recently there had been a coolness between them because Big Aunt suspected, probably justly, that Sister-in-Law Gold Have Got was always complaining about her to Moon Scent, about her injustice, her perpetual nagging.

Way up high on the white wall there were little pictures painted in black ink, a spray of orchids enclosed in a fan-shaped border, and a hexagon framing a sheathed rapier and a stringed instrument—things that were as far removed from their lives as the moon. And the topmost picture, faded by half a century of wind and rain, was faint as a morning moon.

Gold Root finished eating first. He turned his chair around and deliberately, it seemed, sat with his back toward Moon Scent as he hunched forward smoking his long pipe.

SISTER-IN-LAW GOLD HAVE GOT HUNG HER **6** washing on the pock-marked boundary stone, a stone tablet with inscriptions on it, standing about a foot above the ground, outside the house. The limp gray rags flapped a little in the breeze.

"*Ai!* Sister-in-Law Gold Have Got, had your rice?"

She was flustered when she looked up and saw it was Comrade Wong coming this way with a stranger, also in uniform. She was always nervous around Comrade Wong so that he, too, felt apprehensive, never sure that she would say the right thing, though it happened that she did this time.

"*Ai*," she smiled and greeted him back, "you had your rice, too, Comrade Wong?"

But he did not hear her. He hastily covered up whatever it was that she said by calling out loudly, "Very good, very good. And is your father-in-law at home?"

She made her exit hurriedly, shouting, "Comrade Wong has come."

Big Uncle and Big Aunt came out beaming. Wong introduced to them the man in uniform he had brought with him. "This is Comrade Ku," he said. "He has come from Shanghai to study conditions in the country. He wants to lodge with you and live as you live."

They greeted Comrade Ku effusively. Ku was gaunt and thirtyish, wearing dark-rimmed glasses that made his black brows look redundant. He explained that he was a director-writer sent down by the Literary and Artistic Workers' Association to Experience Life and collect material for his next film.

Comrade Small Chang, the militiaman who served as Wong's orderly, panted up from behind them carrying Ku's luggage on a flat-pole. Ku fought with him for the load, trying to take it into the house himself, but Comrade Small Chang refused to part with it. It was his job to deliver the bedroll to the house and he was going to do it. This man from the city, Comrade Ku, had wrestled him all the way, trying to carry his own luggage. In fact, he had almost been tempted to tell this man with the glasses, "Please, Comrade, you stick to your own job, and let me do mine."

Like most villagers, Big Uncle and Big Aunt had had intellectuals staying with them during the Land Reform, so they took it with comparative calm. They were careful not to apologize for the food or the living conditions, or to say, "Did the Comrade come down from Shanghai?" as that would imply that the country was lower than the city.

They showed their guest the room where they kept the millstone and farming implements. These could be cleared out and the door removed from its hinges and set up on two benches to make a bed at night. Ku said it was fine. Then they all returned to the main room and admired the dark blue vase the family had won in the lottery when the landlord's possessions were divided among them.

At Comrade Wong's request, someone ran to fetch Gold Root and his wife. Gold Root was the Labor Model and his wife had only recently returned to the country to join in the productive work. Ku was impressed; these country girls, he thought, could be very pretty. Big Aunt did most of the talking. The others confined themselves to smiling and murmuring, "It is fine now in the country," or "Things are different now." But Big Aunt cried out with gusto, "Without Chairman Mao we would never have this day." And she always referred to him as "Chairman Mao *t'a lao jen chia*," adding on the suffix "big old man of the house," which showed familiarity and affectionate respect, as one might speak of an elder in one's own family.

Ku could see that she was Comrade Wong's prize exhibit. Probably that was why he made him board with her family. When Comrade Wong was leaving, Ku walked him down the road and listened to him talk indulgently of the old woman. "One thing about her— she is very frank and outspoken."

Comrade Wong had already mentioned the Winter School to him and suggested that he go to teach there so as to mingle more with the people. Now he said, "Have a good rest, Comrade. You must be tired after the journey. Tomorrow I'll take you around to the school and introduce you to the class."

Again he enlarged on the importance of teaching the villagers to read and write as a means of Elevating their Political Awareness. To listen to him one would think that this job he was asking Ku to undertake, working in shifts with the schoolboys from the village town, to teach a few characters to illiterate peasants, was the greatest and most challenging work in the whole nation. He was a good propagandist, Ku thought. Wong's "party age" was quite long and he had seen action in northern Kiangsu. He certainly deserved a better post than the one he was holding. Probably it was the infighting between cliques that had kept him down. Perhaps Wong was a follower of some important personage who had been purged by Mao. In that case he would be a dangerous character to associate with. Ku became more wary and withdrawn in his manner.

Comrade Wong walked back alone to his quarters in the Village Public Office, which had formerly been the Temple of the Militant Sage. It wasn't until after he left Ku that he realized he had talked rather a lot about his past—doing underground work during the Japanese occupation, and when things grew too hot for him, running off to join the New Fourth Army. He hadn't meant to bring up all this, not to someone he was meeting for the first time. *Ing-hsiung pu tao tang niun yung.* "Heroes do not boast of their past prowess." It depressed him to think that he was behaving like a garrulous old man living on his memories.

It was the hint of condescension in Ku's attitude to-

ward him that had egged him on. He did not like the
way Ku talked about national and world affairs for his
information, perhaps with the best of intentions, assum-
ing that he was totally ignorant of what was happening
outside the village and must be hungry for news.

He had never heard of this Ku. But he gathered from
the letter of introduction from the head of the Literary
and Artistic Workers' Association that he was a new
recruit to The Cause *after* the Liberation.

"After my twenty years of service to The Party, always
in the thick of the struggle," Wong thought, "here I am
playing host to this miserable turncoat, and being patron-
ized by him—the two-faced, chicken-hearted intellectual—the running dog of the old regime."

He shouldn't lose his temper like this, he knew. And
he was probably being unfair to Ku. The mood hung
heavy over him. He hoped that on returning to the
temple he would find some peasants waiting in his office,
wanting to settle some dispute. It might dispel the gloom.
He knew how to handle peasants and there was always
pleasure in doing a thing well. To the peasants, he *was*
the government. They made him feel he was a vital cog
in the machine instead of an outmoded tool tucked away
in a dark corner.

Usually he was kept busy from morning till night, but
it looked when he got back to the temple as if he was
going to have this afternoon to himself. After sitting at
his desk for a while, he got up and strolled outside, his
hands folded at his back. Comrade Small Chang, who
kept house for him, was sitting outside the door on a
p'u t'uan, the round cushion on which monks sat out
their endless hours of meditation. The monks of this
temple had long been disbanded. And Small Chang was

64

not meditating; he was peeling garlic. The *p'u t'uan* was very old; the straw showed through the torn blue cloth.

Small Chang had their washing hung up to dry on a string drawn across the intricately carved latticed window. A patch of sunlight lay motionless on the dismal, faded pink of the temple wall.

It occurred to Wong that he seemed to be always living in temples, in the semi-darkness of vast, empty halls still haunted by the evicted gods. He was living in a temple when he married Shah Ming. He knew what was coming—whenever he started remembering, that was the part that came most readily to mind.

He had first seen her in a mass meeting of *kan pu* when he was with the New Fourth Army in northern Kiansu. All the *kan pu* gathered in a small town to *sheng ta kê*, attend big class. They made use of the house of an absentee landlord. The great pillared hall was bleak and draughty like the outdoors on a dark day. They sat on the stone-paved floor during the lecture, taking notes on paper pads balanced on their knees. The lecture ended with the shouting of slogans, as all their speeches invariably did. Everybody stood up and repeated after the lecturer, "Long live Chairman Mao!" and tossed his cap into the air, hurling it as high as he could. But not everybody could manage to catch his own headgear when it came down. There was a feverish scrambling for caps as the lecturer again shot up an arm, with his voice straining after it. "Long live Ss Ta-lin!" he shrieked.

"Long live Ss Ta-lin!" echoed the crowd in a deafening yell, and again the caps sailed into the air.

After the meeting broke up, Wong noticed a woman *kan pu* standing there, cap in hand, looking distressed.

65

She had picked up the wrong cap. She was very young. Instead of cutting her hair short like the other women and letting it hang over her cheeks in greasy, stringy locks, she wore it in two braids tucked out of sight under her cap, so that, at first glance, one would have taken her for a boy, with her rather thin, bloodless face and wide-set eyes. But now, with the cap off and the braids showing, she looked very schoolgirlish, fragile, and a bit droopy in the uniform that was too large for her.

Wong took off his frayed and battered cap. It was so obviously his own that he had to dismiss the idea of going up to her and asking her if that was her cap he had picked up by mistake, as some of the other men were doing. None of them had her cap, but on looking around they discovered a cap poised high above on a rafter. A young man named Yu fetched a ladder with great alacrity and retrieved it for her. He was standing there talking to her when Wong left the room. Even the knowledge that Comrade Yu was low in rank and not qualified to marry was small comfort to Wong.

"Who was that girl who lost her cap just now?" he asked another *kan pu* somewhat peevishly. "Such a lot of fuss."

"I've never seen her before. A newcomer. Why, are you interested in her?"

"Don't talk nonsense."

He tried somebody else later on. "That one with the pigtails—is her husband's name Chen?"

"I don't think she is married. You mean Shah Ming, don't you? She came here less than a year ago. Works in the telegraph branch."

"I thought I knew her husband. A Comrade Chen," he mumbled. "I must be mistaken."

The women *kan pu* were lodged for the night in the co-operative store. He went there early next morning and asked for Comrade Shah Ming.

As was the usual arrangement in Chinese shops, there stood on each side of the room a row of carved blackwood chairs with small tables in between, for receiving visitors and important customers. He took a chair. Red scrolls hung on the wall at the back, congratulating the co-operative on its opening.

"A good omen," thought Wong, "proposing to her in a co-operative store. It ought to be the beginning of a lifetime of co-operation in our revolutionary work."

The morning sun streamed in through the door, lighting up the baskets of rice and red beans at his feet, the mounds of dusty mushrooms and *mu ehr*, a kind of fungus like furled black ears, and the large brown peels of bamboo shoots with their dry, sweetish smell. The women *kan pu* chattered loudly at the counter, rolling up their bedding. They had slept on the counter during the night.

Then he saw Shah Ming hurrying toward him. Wong introduced himself. "I want to have a talk with you," he said.

She sat down, smiling, visibly bracing herself. Afterward she told him that she had felt sure he had come to speak to her about her braids, which had occasioned much criticism.

"I heard that you are not married," Wong said. "Neither am I. What do you say if we ask the organization for permission to marry?"

Shah Ming took it very calmly, he thought, though of course she seemed a bit taken aback. She answered, smiling, "*K'ao-liu, k'ao-liu ba!* Let's think it over."

67

"As far as I am concerned, there is no need to reconsider. My mind is made up."

Still she said, smiling, "It is a grave step. *K'ao-liu, k'ao-liu-ba!*"

He did not press her for an immediate decision. It affected him strangely to see her in the sunlight—she had the quality of a yellowed photograph, looking so young and yet faded. He felt as though he must be careful not to touch the picture with his finger, lest it would fade more.

Two weeks later he visited her at her post. She had to wake up a colleague on the night shift to do her work for her while she came out to talk to him.

"Let's send in the petition," he suggested. "If either of us is unfit to marry, you can depend on it that the organization will tell us so. We can safely leave that to the organization."

She kept putting him off with her *"K'ao-liu, k'ao-liu ba!"* But the second time he came to see her at her post she gave in and said reluctantly, "All right." So they sent in the petition and were granted permission to marry. One evening Wong dispatched an orderly to fetch her on horseback.

The clockety-clock of the horse's hoofs sounded sharp and clear in the evening quiet. He waited on the stone steps outside the temple until the sound had faded away in the distance, then he went in. The hall was dark except for the lamplight coming from his room. He could just distinguish the blue faces and red faces of a row of minor gods down one side, and their gilded draperies. Gusts of wind made the tattered paper on the windows flap loudly. He crossed the hall and went into the eastern chamber, which was his room. Today the

68

room had been swept and tidied up, so that it looked very empty.

The war years had been a period of compromise for The Party, so the idols had been left intact in this temple they occupied and the nuns allowed to remain, though the young ones had all run away. An old nun who stayed on was "doing her lessons" at the back of the temple, beating a wooden *mu yu*. It went on and on, an even flow of "toc toc toc toc," like water dripping from an ancient water clock, marking time for a dead world.

Wong felt the spell come over him as he paced about his room, waiting for the girl. She came that night, and left at dawn on the same horse, with the orderly holding the reins for her. After that he sent for her every week. Invariably she came at night and left at dawn, like a ghost mistress in those old stories.

At times he almost struggled against the spell. He would have liked to think of her as a part of his everyday life, like other men's wives. The only time he ever felt really married to her was when there was an emergency meeting of the *kan pu* in the country town where he was stationed. The Communists had always placed great importance on the decoration of places where meetings were going to be held. A high-ranking official would inspect the room personally before the meeting and rage at the *kan pu* in charge if the vase of flowers on the table on the platform was not just so. But in this devastated area there were no flowers to be had, or flags and streamers and suitable lighting effects. Wong had failed even to obtain a large portrait of Mao Tze-tung, which was essential.

Shah Ming solved the problem by pasting a large sheet of red paper in the center of the wall, with "Long live

Chairman Mao" written on it in big black characters. Then she took two brass basins, the kind that everybody used around here, filled them with cooking oil, and set them on the table, one on each side. During the meeting, when the oil was lit, it made a most impressive scene, with the huge, pulsating orange flames, the light and shadows playing on the red paper in the background, and all the *kan pu* holding up an arm, swearing allegiance to The Party.

Wong was immensely proud of his wife, feeling just as if they had given a successful party. Afterward he enjoyed talking over everything with her, the mishaps as well as the amusing incidents. It was wonderful when all the guests departed and she did not leave with them, but stayed with him for the night.

She told him how she had come to join the New Fourth Army. During her senior year in high school she had been befriended by a woman teacher who was a Communist. It was most exciting, the whispered midnight talks, the surreptitious reading of propaganda literature by the light of a candle, behind the padded blanket. The teacher told her Russia was the only country who really helped China to fight the Japanese invaders. She kept her informed of the newest victories Yenan scored against the Japanese. Shah Ming became a convert along with several other girls and the teacher took them with her when she escaped from the Japanese-held areas into northern Kiangsu, where the New Fourth Army operated.

Shah Ming, Bright Sand, was a name she adopted after she came here. It was mannish and smart, rather like a fashionable pen name or stage name.

She told him about the last house they were stationed

in. The four telegraphers, one young man and three girls, occupied the living room in a peasant's house. At night they slept on the tables they worked at in the daytime. There was no door—it had been cut up for firewood by marauding soldiers. The north wind blew straight in, making it extremely difficult to keep the oil lamp alight. But even then it was warmer indoors than in the cowshed, so the farmer always took his buffalo into the living room at night and tied it to the window frame. Whenever the buffalo started to urinate, one of the telegraphers on the night shift had to jump up from her seat, dash over, and set the pail under it, then return to her work. Again, when it had finished, one of them had to go over and remove the pail immediately, otherwise the beast was sure to kick it over and flood the floor.

In a way it was a blessing to have the buffalo in the room. She could recall freezing nights when the three girls cuddled up to sleep under the buffalo's belly, like calves.

She told him all this a bit shamefacedly, and together they laughed at her predicaments.

"It is a painful experience," he admitted, "the petty bourgeois throwing himself into the furnace of revolution. But this is how we are remade."

He felt sorry for her, but the most he allowed himself to say was, "You'll be able to stand it better if you have better health. But don't worry, your health will improve."

In early summer she fell ill from a miscarriage and was laid on an unhinged door, the only kind of stretcher available in the countryside, and carried to the temple, where there was a medical-aid station for wounded soldiers. Wong was glad to have her with him, though he had no time to nurse her. They were suffering military reverses, and the day came when they had to evacuate the place in a hurry.

The order came in the small hours before dawn, throwing everybody into a frenzy of activity. The soldiers had to return everything they borrowed from the peasants, since their slogan was "Not a needle, not a thread from the people." They could be heard everywhere noisily pounding on doors and shouting, "*Ta niung! Ta niung!* Aunt! Aunt!" An old peasant woman, roused from her sleep, would open the door fearfully. The soldier would hand over a battered rice pot with a hole at the bottom, or a broken chair, and thank her for lending it to them for the past six months.

"We are leaving now. But don't worry, *ta niung,*" he would say soothingly, "we are coming back."

Wong had a million things to attend to. Hurrying back to their quarters, he found that Shah Ming had forced herself to sit up in bed and pack her belongings into a small bundle. For a moment he felt distressed, not knowing how to tell her that she was not going with him.

"It's going to be a rough trip." He sat down on the bed and turned to face her, his palms on his knees, authoritatively. "It's better for your health if you don't come along. I have arranged with Comrade Fang to have you stay with his parents for the time being." Comrade Fang was his orderly. Wong knew he could count on the loyalty of the parents so long as he had the son with him as hostage.

She went on slowly with her packing, though eventually she stopped and bent forward as if exhausted, pressing her face against the bundle in her lap. He knew she was crying.

"It's a very common thing," he said. "Comrades often have to stay in enemy territory and go under cover."

"I want to come with you," she sobbed.

"But there aren't enough stretchers," he blurted out, "or stretcher-bearers. And we have to take all the wounded soldiers with us. You can easily escape notice. But what chance has a wounded man got?"

He had his own packing to do. Presently, when he turned to her again, he saw that she had stopped crying and had continued with her packing. The cocks were crowing and the yellow light of the oil lamp grew bleak, diluted by the gray daylight. He felt as if they were catching an early train.

Comrade Fang's father and brother came, carrying an unhinged door. They helped her onto it and covered her up with a padded blanket, though it was June. Sick people were always supposed to keep warm. Wong bent down to tuck in the blanket around her neck and whispered, "You'll be all right. But be careful all the same. And get well quick. We'll be back here soon." She nodded slightly on the pillow, her face damp and pale.

"Don't worry, Comrade. Everything will be all right," the old man said loudly, though he was obviously heavy-hearted in anticipation of the troubles and danger thus thrust upon him. The forced cheerfulness in his tone struck a chilly note in Wong's heart as he watched them carrying her across the rice paddies, under the morning stars.

The army moved to another district. This was toward the end of the war, when all sides had grown tired and cynical. When any one side girded itself for a fresh effort and surged forward, the other side simply surrendered *en masse*, only to break away at the first opportunity. The situation became positively farcical, with whole battalions being pushed back and forth between the opposing commanders like big piles of chips on a gambling table.

Under the circumstances there was always considerable traffic across the borders. But as time went on, it became apparent that Shah Ming had lost touch with the New Fourth Army. Lots of things could have happened. She might have been discovered or betrayed, and she could have died from her illness or the lack of medical care.

Once Wong managed to send somebody to the Fangs to deliver a letter from their son, asking them about Shah Ming. According to the Fangs, they had sent her away to stay with a relative of theirs in another village some distance away, because she was known in this district and was in danger of being identified. But they heard that she had already left there of her own free will.

Finally Wong had an opportunity to go there himself to investigate. Disguised as a small tradesman, he went to the village indicated by the Fangs and asked for their relative, known as Chow Pa-kê, Eighth Brother Chow.

Chow Pa-kê was a short little man around forty with protuberant eyes and closely shaved, greenish scalp. His head, perfectly round to begin with, somehow looked battered and out of shape. And he was chinless out of self-defense, so that nobody could deal him a knockout blow on the chin.

Poised and well-mannered in his long gown of blue cotton, he was no ordinary farmer but had often dabbled in business and knew all about lumber, silkworms, salt, tea, and taxes. Wong pretended that he was interested in lumber and had been directed by the Fangs to ask for information from Chow Pa-kê, since he was on the way here. Chow turned out to be so eloquent that Wong thought his name Pa-kê must be a nickname, as *pa-kê* is also Chinese for parakeet, a kind of bird which could learn to talk with great facility and was known for its cleverness. But in time Chow's wife appeared and was addressed by others as "Eighth Sister-in-Law." So *Pa-kê* stood for Eighth Brother, after all.

Chow pressed him to stay for lunch. During the meal, his host initiated him into the complexities of taxation, the various authorities along the way who had to be appeased, and the soldiers he was likely to come across. This was one of those unfortunate areas which were alternately raided by the Japanese, the Communists, the Peace Army of the puppet government, and all sorts of nondescript troops who owed nominal allegiance to the government in Chungking.

They had a few cups of wine together and Chow told him about "that time the Japanese came down from Tungchow."

"Walked right into the house," he said. "The officer who headed the party asked me, 'You are *lao-pai-shing*, common civilian?' And I said 'Yes.' So then he asked me, 'You like Chinese soldiers or Japanese soldiers?' I didn't know what was the best way to answer the question. I didn't know whether he was Chinese or Japanese. He was speaking Chinese all right."

"But surely you can tell by the accent," said Wong. Then he remembered that, to the peasants, soldiers all sounded alike, just as outlandish, whether it was a Japanese speaking Chinese or a Chinese northerner speaking Mandarin.

"*Ai*," said Chow, without pausing, "you can't tell by

75

the accent either. The only way to tell is by their boots. *Ai!* Quite different. But I didn't dare look." He made as if he was standing at attention, raising his head a little and stiffening his neck. Then with a smile and a slight shake of his head, he said, "Didn't dare look downward."

Wong said patiently, "Yes, I suppose it seems rude to look people up and down."

"So then how did I answer him? I sighed and said, '*Ai-yah, hsien-hseng,* mister! We *lao-pai-shing* really have a hard life! Whenever we see soldiers, whether they are Chinese or Japanese, it's all the same to us. All we want is some peace—it's best for everybody all round.' And he said, 'You are right.' So then I knew he was a Japanese," he concluded, well pleased with himself.

After lunch Wong got up to leave. Having made sure that Wong was setting out immediately for a neighboring town and had to be there before nightfall, Chow expressed his regrets that he could not lodge with them for a few days.

"Your generosity overwhelms me," said Wong. "Though I've already heard a lot about your hospitality. That reminds me—I have a relative, a young lady, I heard she also lodged with you when she passed this place. I forgot even to thank you."

"Which young lady?" Chow asked after a slight pause.

"She was staying with the Fangs," said Wong, regarding him intently.

Chow went quite blank. "You must be mistaken. We didn't have any young lady visiting us."

She could have disguised her age. "Well, I've always thought of her as being young," Wong said, laughing, "maybe because when I last saw her she was a mere chit of a girl. Actually, she must be getting on. Middle-aged, you might say."

"No," Chow said, "no middle-aged lady came to my house."

"I heard she has aged terribly with her illness. She must look quite old."

"No old lady either," Chow said firmly.

Wong was well aware that the other's reticence might be due to the fear that he was an agent from any of the other sides on the track of a woman Communist. So Wong did a reckless thing and revealed himself.

"Don't be afraid to speak the truth," he said. "I represent the New Fourth Army. You can safely tell me exactly what happened. If you hide anything, it is at your own peril."

Chow was in a quandary. The man pronounced himself a Communist but there was no telling which side he really belonged to. This time it wouldn't help even to look at his boots, as he wore none, being in civilian clothes.

Chow fenced for time and continued to deny having seen a lady of any age cross his threshold.

"The Fangs said they sent her to you. What have you done to her? Turned her over the gendarmes?" pressed Wong.

"*Lao-tien-yae*, Old Lord Heaven, I know nothing about this! The Fangs are lying, if that's what they said. *Ai-yah*, why do they do this to me?"

"You've sent one of our people to her death and you'll pay for it," said Wong.

After a lot of threatening, Chow finally broke down and admitted that he had given shelter to a girl who was ill. If in the end Wong turned out to be an agent from another side, he could always say he had been forced to make up the story, seeing that was the only way to get rid of the man.

"Where is she now?" Wong asked.

"She left us in the eighth moon. She said she was going to Chinkiang to get into a hospital. She had relatives there, she said."

"She went by herself?"

"She was much better when she left. She said she could make the trip alone."

Wong asked other questions but that was about all he could get out of Chow. He was inclined to believe him, because the girl did have an uncle in Chinkiang.

Wong went back to his post reasonably happy. But soon other doubts assailed him. Why hadn't she communicated with him or any of their associates if she was in a city like Chinkiang where it was comparatively easy to make contacts?

Later there had been rumors of her being seen in Chinkiang. As her defection from The Cause became increasingly evident, her name sometimes came up in discussions, and all Wong could say was, "It's a pity her standing ground is not firm. But then the petty bourgeois as a class has always been vacillating and unreliable. I am sorry I haven't been able to influence her."

He wondered for the first time whether she had been happy with him. Since their union was not recognized by the outside world, there was every possibility that she had married somebody else and settled down to the humdrum life of a small-town housewife. And Wong told himself that, personal feelings aside, he wished fervently that she would return to The Revolution, for her own sake. In those times of stress, the organization was not over-particular. Deserters were always taken back, after the proper show of repentance.

Wong was with the troops when they were marching into a town at nightfall. The town had changed hands many times and had been the scene of many battles. Passing the water front, the straggly column stepped onto a deserted, pebble-paved street flanked on both sides by jagged white ruins. They were very tall for two-storied houses, being high-ceilinged. Wong happened to glance up as he marched past a roofless house with eyeless black holes for windows. It gave him quite a jolt to see a girl looking down at him from a window on the second floor. He had no idea those houses were still habitable.

Though the girl's face was little more than a white blur in the deepening dusk, it could be seen that she was pretty, and, to his astonishment, she seemed to be smiling at him. He looked away, thinking that he knew what kind of house this was; but these sluts should have known that they couldn't do business with the New Fourth Army. Then, with a start, he looked up again when an inner voice shouted, "Shah Ming! Why, it's Shah Ming!" But the face had vanished, almost as if the sudden clamor within him had reached her ears and had frightened her away.

Stepping out of the ranks, he stood staring up at the window. Was she avoiding him? But she was smiling at him just now. She must be hurrying down the pitch-black, rickety staircase. She would stumble and fall and break her neck. He found a rectangular opening that had once been the door and stepped quickly inside.

For a moment he felt confused, not knowing what had happened. A cool breeze fanned his cheeks. Black shapes loomed around him but there was a dim, mauvish blue light overhead. There seemed to be crickets singing squeakily underfoot. He was standing outdoors. The whole house had been blown up except the façade, behind which there was nothing but rubble.

His eyes sought the second-story window where he had seen the girl, the first window from the left—that would be the first window from the right, in reverse. It was merely a rectangular hole in the lonely white wall that stood jagged against the evening sky. His scalp felt cold and tightly drawn as he looked into the dusky void of the window, where the stars were beginning to appear.

He could hear the rhythmical thud-thud of the soldiers marching far down the empty street. At the sound of those retreating footsteps, Wong suddenly went wild with fear. He tore into the street and ran all the way to catch up with them.

While it had been a shattering experience, it also filled him with a kind of elation. He was convinced that she had appeared to him because she wanted him to know that she was dead. She did not want him to think that she had been unfaithful to him.

Then his training stepped in and told him that that was mere superstition. And he was forced to the conclusion that, on top of losing her, he was losing his sanity.

Years passed before he heard anything definite about her. In the course of being shifted about after the Communist occupation of the whole of China, he came across an old colleague who used to know them both. The man told him that he had seen Shah Ming in Soochow. She showed no recognition of him when they met, so he did not greet her. But later he had made inquiries and had learned that she was now married, had two children, and cwned a shop selling wicker furniture and straw slippers. Wong wasn't much affected by the news. Emotional exhaustion had long reconciled him to the thought that she was still alive, bearing children and growing old in another man's house.

He had an opportunity to visit his home village for the first time in nineteen years. His mother still lived but they no longer had anything in common. All she had to tell him was endless tales of woe, of losses and privations, and all his assurances of better days to come failed to cheer her. His family had previously made arrangements for his marriage, taking the girl into their house when they were both children. They worked her harder than a slave girl throughout the years and she had become quite a hag. Wong did the right thing by her and married her. But every time he went home for a visit, which was very seldom, he felt lonelier than ever.

While he had no close friends, he had always got on well enough with everybody, with the exception of his superiors. Consequently, he was always the one who got criticized and blamed whenever anything went wrong. During meetings, even when he came out well in an argument, the summing up by the presiding official would twist things to his disadvantage. There was no promotion for him after the Communists took over the country. Instead, he was labeled "unable to keep pace with changing situations." Being a *kan pu* was a lifetime job, however, so like many other veteran *kan pu* he was pensioned off with a small post in the country.

He had no quarrel with the over-all policy of The Party. He had been trained to accept it unquestioningly. It was the small things that jarred him—the officials' wives holding sinecures; the importance of knowing the right people, of *chao kuan hsi,* finding connections. And he was appalled by what seemed to him to be rank extravagance, like rebuilding the temples in all their splendor in Peking and Shanghai, just to impress Tibetan delegates on a visit. He knew where all this money came from. He personally had to get it out of the peasants.

He often got angry, but his was the helpless fury of lonely old people slighted by their only friends. He never sulked for long, but always came round of his own accord. The Party was all he had left in the world.

TEACHING AT THE WINTER SCHOOL PROVED **7**
to be more strenuous than Ku expected. The
schoolhouse was five miles away and he was not used to
walking. Besides, he was hungry. Even when he had
been there a week, after puffing up the path against the
choking north wind he felt so faint when he stood at the
blackboard that he kept dropping the chalk.

The food was shocking. He came to the country grimly
prepared for anything but this. Various friends who had
gone out in the country to help in the Land Reform had
given him advice with an ill-concealed air of superiority.
"The farmer is naïve," they said. "When he feels friendly
toward you he might offer you a sesame cake he has al-

ready bitten on. Be sure to eat it up. Again, the farmer's wife might wipe a chair with the same cloth she had just dried the baby's bottom with and ask you to sit down. You must not hesitate and hurt her feelings." He did not find the farmers as naïve as they were pictured. And where were the sesame cakes? All they had here was a watery gruel with inch-long sections of grass floating in it.

Of course he could not speak to anybody about the matter, and least of all to Comrade Wong. So he had no means of finding out whether the situation was only local or spread over a large area. He could find no mention in the newspapers of famine in this or any other part of the country. He had a curious sensation of having dropped out of time and space, living nowhere.

The strange dull, gnawing sense of hunger, something new to him—a cross between toothache and heartache—made everything else seem unreal, the sunny fields, the woodcutters on the hillside, the sound of distant gongs and cymbals in the wind—the people in the Rice-Sprout Song Corps had been called out to practice again and were dancing and wriggling under the eye of the cultural cadre.

It was incredible how the people carried on as usual. They cooked three times a day. In the damp air the blue wood smoke hung around for a long time with its clean, acrid fragrance. At noon, all over the countryside the black-roofed white houses issued smoke from square holes in their walls. Slowly it poured out like the soul leaving the body and melting away in a moment of holy ecstasy. Watching it, somehow Ku thought of an oft-quoted saying of Confucius or some other sage, "To the people, food is God." Watching the wood smoke trailing off into the air from the stoves under the pots of thin rice gruel, he thought, how can they go on like this, when food is God to them?

He was afraid that he was losing weight. That worried him most. Everybody who participated in the Land Reform boasted of having grown fat after three months in the country. Some claimed they had been cured of all kinds of illnesses of long standing. To those who hung back from the dreaded ordeal they would say, "It is a hard life but you can grow fat, if your Thought has already been Straightened Out." On the other hand, growing thin would indicate inner conflict, resistance in the subconscious mind. Ku wondered how he was going to face his friends and colleagues. Two or three months of this, and he would be thin as a scarecrow. And he could not blame it on the famine. That he could never mention to anybody, unless he wanted to run the risk of being arrested as a Nationalist spy spreading malicious rumors.

It would seem, he told himself, rather admiring his own sense of satire, that in the matter of ill-nourishment and long working hours The Party Comrades departed from their materialistic standpoint and became extreme spiritualists, forever asserting the superiority of mind over matter. Bitterly, Ku recalled the much-publicized case of Miss Totally Fragrant Fu, the famous Shaoshing opera actress and a beautiful consumptive, who had taken part in the Land Reform. She wrote to all her friends giving glowing accounts of how her health improved under the trying circumstances. She said she had served as an errand boy and trudged thirty miles on straw sandals in snow two feet deep, to deliver a letter. Now she could eat three huge bowls of rice every meal and had gained twenty pounds. Three bowls of rice! Ku felt that he could do with three huge bowls of rice himself.

He tried to work in spite of this craving obsession. He was searching for story material that might be interpreted in such a way as to throw light on the flourishing and progressive state of the peasantry after the Land Reform. In his heart he still maintained that the country must be prospering, "as a whole." He found that a very useful phrase.

He talked with various persons. Comrade Wong accompanied him to some of the neighboring villages to visit the soldiers' families. The people were very pleasant but they never had much to say. On the other hand, there were quite a few who talked too much, probably under the impression that he was some visiting dignitary who had the power to improve their lot. In halting, mumbled phrases they would intimate that they were actually worse off than before. To handle such cases Ku had discovered the simple expedient of dismissing them as "not typical."

Comrade Wong would probably call Big Aunt "typical." But Comrade Wong had never lived with her and did not know her intoning of those set phrases could get to be very monotonous. Sometimes Ku could almost believe that she was a shameless liar. He interviewed Gold Root T'an and his wife. They both seemed shy, but Ku still had hopes that when they grew more used to him they might open up.

Gold Root took the Winter School seriously. Moon Scent also went regularly because her husband seemed to like it. She learned the tunes of some of the songs they taught there, "The East Is Red" and "Beat Down the American Wolves." But she paid little attention to the lessons. She was not interested in self-improvement. Like all women who are happy in their marriage, she felt immensely complacent.

86

Gold Root went and asked Ku to write out the characters for "door," "table," "chair," all those things around the house, for him to cut out and paste on the actual object. Everybody crowded around Ku's door to watch him wield the brush. Moon Scent also came peering, standing on tiptoe with an arm around the neck of Sister-in-Law Gold Have Got.

Then she said, "*Ai*, Sister-in-Law Gold Have Got, with a teacher right in your house you should really be ashamed if you do not learn your lessons!" She gave the older woman a push and ran away laughing.

Sister-in-Law Gold Have Got blushed and smiled confusedly because nobody ever joked with her. And Ku looked up at this with a smile. Sometimes this pretty country woman could be bold, too, he thought.

He ought to be able to build a story around her. She was a true daughter of the soil, unspoiled by her stay in the city. She had come back in answer to the call of "Return to the Land," and he noticed that she seemed happier than most other people around here.

One day when he returned from a stroll he saw her hanging up her washing on a tree. There were some children's underpants made of an old cotton print of a pinkish red color which looked well on the high branches. The tree seemed bright with flowers in midwinter. She was not tall but she was sturdily built. Ku found himself wondering what she was like in summer without those wadded clothes that made every woman look pregnant. The padded pants folded right over the stomach, pushing the jacket well out.

"The winter is colder here than in Shanghai," he said.

She agreed with him pleasantly. He sat down on the boundary stone nearby, and asked her where she used to

87

live when she was in Shanghai. It turned out to be not far from his place. She remarked that it was a convenience to have the market only a few blocks away.

She seemed singularly accessible today. As they went on talking she asked him how many people there were in his family, how many servants, and if they had the house to themselves and whether they had many friends and relations in Shanghai. With a shock he came to realize that she was working around to sounding him out on the possibility of his getting her a job in the city, and also help her husband to find one if possible.

After that he never approached her again.

He wrote regularly to his wife and friends and walked thirty miles to the village town to post the letters. Afterward he would have lunch in a restaurant—rice or noodles with eggs, meat, bean-curd skin, vegetables, and bamboo shoots. He looked forward to those trips with increasing impatience. Then one day Comrade Wong dropped in to ask him if he had any letters to post. Comrade Wong was going to town for a meeting and could mail them for him.

He found himself trembling with anger. So they wanted to deprive him even of this one full meal in days. Then he pulled himself together. There was every possibility of Wong having spied on him while he was in town but Wong probably would not object to his eating a good meal out of his own pocket, though he might despise him for it.

"No, I don't have any letters to mail," he said, smiling. Luckily the one he wrote last night had a book lying on top of it on the table to press down the flap of the envelope. The glue never stuck since it went down in price to Face the Masses.

It was crazy, his telling a lie like that. If Wong happened to take up that book and see the letter he would certainly think it held some secret. Otherwise, why should he be afraid to trust it to anybody else?

He must get Wong away from this room as soon as possible.

"The New Year is coming; you must be homesick," Wong said jocularly, slapping him on the back. "Miss your lover?" He used the accepted Communist term for wife.

Ku smiled. "Comrade Wong, are you going home to see your lover during the New Year?"

"I have not been home for two years," Wong said, smiling. "You know how it is. There never is time."

"Comrade Wong, you are too ardent in serving the people. And you are always so busy from morning till night. I never have a chance to learn from you."

"You are too modest. There is no need to be modest when you are among your own comrades."

"No, but there are many things I want to consult you about. If you are going to town this morning, suppose I walk you to the Temple of the Earth God? We can talk on the way."

"Yes—in fact, I should have started before now."

Comrade Small Chang was waiting for Wong outside the house. The local militia wore no uniform, and for arms most of them had to make do with rods, swords, and lances. But Small Chang carried a rifle. They made an impressive showing as they strolled out of the village with their bodyguard bringing up the rear.

Comrade Wong asked Ku how he was getting on with his story, and observed, as he had done on several previous occasions, "You should have been here during the

Land Reform. Let me tell you—it was a truly inspiring experience."

Ku resented having this thrown in his face all the time—that he did not volunteer his services during the Land Reform. It had been a particularly severe winter and his wife had worried about his lungs. Of course he knew exactly what Wong thought of him—a latecomer to the scene, purely an opportunist.

"Truly inspiring. You should have seen the look of sheer joy in the farmers' eyes when they had the landlord's farming implements divided among them," Wong said.

"But that kind of joy is out of date now," Ku said testily. "The *Literary Journal* had a special article about it last month. It says writers are not to dwell on the happiness of the farmers after the Land Reform. That must only be a passing phase. It is time to move up a step."

Wong listened carefully, with the proper respect for the leading magazine of the nation. "Yes, that is true," he said guardedly. "There is still lots of work to be done."

"The *Literary Journal* has lashed out at the present state of mind in the countryside. It says the Turned Over Farmers think only of eating and drinking. They have dreams of *sun-changfa chia,* Produce-and-Build-up-a Family Fortune. Up north they made up a jingle which sums up their ideal:

"THIRTY ACRES AND A BUFFALO,
A WIFE AND BABY AND A WARM BED."

"Yes, yes—they lacked Political Awareness," Comrade Wong agreed.

" 'And if they own a pig they want to slaughter it and have a feast when their daughter marries,' " Ku went on quoting.

Wong nodded regretfully. "Yes, the farmers are still backward. Their Political Awareness needs Elevating." They both fell into these familiar phrases without hesitation.

"How is your organization of Mutual Help Units getting on?"

"Oh, our Harvesting Corps worked very well this autumn," Wong said brightly. "And next spring we plan to turn the Harvesting Corps into Co-operative Units. The union will be much closer. You see, all the buffaloes will be concentrated and redistributed to different units. The men will go into the fields collectively, at the toot of a whistle."

Ku was not really interested in those first steps toward collectivization, the painful process of weaning the peasant from the land he had just received. He knew better than to tackle such a subject in his film. There was always the danger that he would over-emphasize the reluctance of the farmers to join such units and make it look as if they were antagonistic to the government. That would be fatal.

Though he was cheerful and fluent on the subject Wong was probably more worried than he would care to admit. They had come to the mouth of the village when suddenly the stream shone bright ahead of them. They walked on the bank of the stream and Wong sighed.

"It is not easy, Comrade, doing political work," he said. "How I envy you Literary and Artistic Workers. In this great age there are so many stirring events crying to be written about and told to the people. All that was taboo under the reactionary government can now be told. Everywhere you look you see a story."

Ku agreed that this was indeed a great age.

"I used to write myself when I was young," Wong said wistfully.

Ku could imagine what kind of things Comrade Wong had written as a budding Communist for the school magazine. But he listened politely to Wong telling him how he used to contribute to and then edited the local newspaper in a town in Kiangsi.

In winter the water was shallow, revealing piles of gray stones in the middle of the stream. Ku thought it looked like a concrete road under repair.

It was then that he got his great idea for the story of the dam. Suppose that the stream overflowed every year, flooding the fields and wiping out part of the crop. Well, let's make the engineer from the city and some old farmers put their heads together and solve the problem by building a dam with a door. This would serve to illustrate the union of technical knowledge and peasant wisdom. If the engineer thought it up all by himself he, of course, would be guilty of the Self-glorification of the Intellectual. And if the old farmers refused to co-operate, relying only on their past experiences, they were guilty of Experiencism. This idea would avoid both.

There had been numerous films about the engineer and the old factory workers putting their heads together and working wonders. They would repair a burst boiler, prolong the life of an old worn-out lathe, manufacture for a cotton mill an important spare part that was previously imported from America and could not be replaced. But hitherto the situation had never been applied to the farming population. He had opened up a whole new vista.

In his excitement he cast aside his usual reserve and asked Wong as soon as the latter came to a pause in his literary reminiscences, "Comrade Wong, is there a dam anywhere near here?"

"A dam?" Wong was taken aback, his story about the newspaper choked off in midstream. "No. But why? You want to see a dam?" From the sudden interest that lit up his eyes and widened his smile, Ku could see that he had become suspicious.

"No, I was just thinking, would it help to build a dam here if the stream overflows in summer and floods the fields?"

"It does not overflow."

"But suppose it does," Ku explained. "I was just thinking I might build up a story around that."

"Yes, but——" Wong stared at him in amazement. "Why would you want to make one up, when there is so much story material around, in this great age? Besides—it does not overflow." At last he had Ku sized up as that kind of writer. He opened his mouth to laugh and checked himself just in time. But a great flock of ducks suddenly burst into sight and floated downstream incredibly fast, cackling madly with an elderly glee. It was as if, through a brilliant feat of ventriloquism, his laughter was transplanted and borne swiftly downstream. It left him and Ku both somewhat out of countenance.

THE WEATHER WAS FAR TOO WARM FOR **8**
winter. Probably it would rain. A cloud of
tiny winged insects whirled round and round a tree.
From where Moon Scent stood it looked as if the treetop
were smoking.

Somebody was beating a small gong from one end of
the village to the other, shouting, "A meeting! Go to the
Village Public Office for the meeting! Everybody has
to go!"

Moon Scent had to take the child with her since there
would be nobody at home. Leading Beckon by the hand,
she went next door to pick up Sister-in-Law Gold Have
Got. Gold Root went by himself. On such occasions the

men and women always went separately. At the meeting they would also be grouped by themselves although there really was no segregation rule.

The Village Public Office had formerly been the Temple of the Militant Sage. Meetings took place in the great stone-paved courtyard facing the main hall. The villagers pushed about, shouting across at their acquaintances and squinting in the afternoon sunlight. When the Chairman of the Farmers' Association slapped a piece of bamboo on the table, a hush fell upon the gathering and one could hear cocks crowing dreamily in the distance before he cleared his throat and started speaking.

Moon Scent was not yet used to those meetings, which seemed to take more of her time than they had in the city. She was always the last to raise her hand when the time came for everybody to hold up his hand. The women would titter a little while doing it and the men in almost equal shyness carefully kept their eyes front, with a half-smile and a look that said: "Maybe this is simply a ritual. But silly as it seems, it is the thing to do."

Then Gold Root stood up at the back and said, "I move that we ask Comrade Wong to tell us his ideas." The Chairman of the Farmers' Association started to clap and after a while the people caught on and all joined in. Moon Scent's heart beat fast. Nobody clapped when others stood up to speak, but as soon as Gold Root opened his mouth they all applauded. But should she do the same? She would be the village laughingstock—a wife clapping at her own husband. But, on the other hand, she was afraid to be the only dissenter. She was still in the agony of indecision when the clapping stopped and Comrade Wong walked up the stone steps and addressed the crowd.

He made a very long speech about Cultural Entertainment Activities, more to impress Ku than for the edification of the villagers. It was already getting dark when he introduced Ku to them and asked him to give a talk on the same subject. The audience had stood on their feet so long by this time that even their arms ached from hanging down at their sides.

Ku mercifully made his speech short. After the meeting broke up they practiced the Dance of the Rice-Sprout Song outside the temple. Lanterns and torches cast a flickering light on the red walls. The dancers banged the gongs and clashed their cymbals.

> "CHONG! CHONG! CHI-CHONG CHI!
> CHONG! CHONG! CHI-CHONG CHI!"

The young men, Gold Root among them, bound yellow kerchiefs tight on their heads, pulling up the corners of their eyes and eyebrows, turning them into warlike and fearsome strangers. They started dancing, swinging their arms as they advanced and retreated. The others looked on, smiling. But a heaving and pushing began among the spectators, and more and more people were pushed out, under protest, to join the row of dancers.

A woman whose turn it was to be victimized dragged Moon Scent with her, shouting, "You come, too, Sister-in-Law Gold Root." Moon Scent giggled and put up a struggle but was finally induced to stand in line. She had never danced and her ancestors had not danced for more than a thousand years in this part of the country. She felt ridiculous even if she had seen schoolgirls and factory girls prancing the same dance on the street in Shanghai and conceded that it must be a stylish thing to do.

Finally the torches were extinguished and the lanterns

walked off with their owners. Everybody went home. Moon Scent felt the sweat drip cold inside her wadded jacket and was so weak from fatigue and lack of supper that she felt lightheaded. She had always liked crowds. She walked beside Sister-in-Law Gold Have Got, holding Beckon by the hand. In the dark she could hear Gold Root's voice talking to other men some distance away. It gave her a comforting and glad sense of possession to hear his voice even if she couldn't see him.

The moon was behind the clouds. Layers of clouds formed a rocky cave with an amber glow at the rim. Then it started to drizzle. The moon was still there, a fairy light in the amber cave. But before they reached home it was raining hard and they had to run for shelter.

Gold Root had come back ahead of her. The lamp still smoked a bit from just having been lit.

"You could have helped me to carry Beckon," Moon Scent complained. "Heavy as a big rock. I'm all out of breath."

"I did not see you."

She had scarcely sat down when somebody was pounding the door from outside.

"Who is it?" Gold Root went up to the door and shouted above the clatter of the rain on the roof.

It was Sister-in-Law Gold Have Got, coming to borrow a basin or an earthen jar. "The roof is leaking in Comrade Ku's room," she said. "We don't have enough containers to hold the water. All his things are getting wet."

Moon Scent helped her to lug a big earthen jar to her place and saw the state of confusion things were in. Ku's belongings were all stacked in Big Aunt's room and the family were discussing sleeping arrangements. Moon

Scent told Gold Root what was wrong when she came back, and Gold Root went over to ask Comrade Ku to stay the night with them. The old couple frowned and grinned at the same time, trying not to look overjoyed.

"All right then," Big Aunt said reluctantly. "He might stay with you for a few days while we repair our roof. But we'll fix it as quickly as possible."

But still Big Aunt dared not pass Ku on to her nephew without consulting Comrade Wong. Big Uncle put on his hobnail boots, and with his lantern and umbrella went out in the downpour to see Comrade Wong at his quarters in the temple. Having obtained Wong's consent, they started moving the luggage. Moon Scent swept the room formerly occupied by Gold Flower. Big Aunt helped to spread out Ku's bedding, her widowed daughter-in-law being ineligible for such intimate service. The whole family came over to see that he was well settled. Ku was just as happy as they were at being moved and just as anxious not to show it. Beckon circled around his possessions, putting out her hand to touch everything. She was bold because Ku had always been specially nice to her out of all the children.

At last Big Uncle and Big Aunt got up to go, with Sister-in-Law Gold Have Got holding their umbrella for them. They cursed and laughed at the rain. Already their voices were louder, they even coughed more loudly with their guest gone. It was now Gold Root and his wife's turn to whisper. Ku could hear them talking softly in the next room as if they had a sick man with them. Now and then the child's voice piped up, shrill and uninhibited.

He sat on the bed facing the oil lamp, and was suddenly filled with longing for his own home and wife. He moved the tubular bamboo lampstand farther away to make room on the table. Then he spread out his letter paper and wrote to his wife. He told her how he had moved house tonight to escape from the leaky roof, how affectionate the farmers were, how touching their concern. He spoke of his work in the Winter School and reported the talk he gave this evening on Cultural Entertainment Activities.

The wind was one long level howl on the horizon. The bamboo partition rattled loudly. In the other half of the room, partitioned off, Big Uncle's pig grunted uneasily, because of the noise of the wind and rain and because it was not used to the lamplight that leaked through, falling in long stripes across the floor.

Ku stopped writing to warm his numb fingers at the small flame of the lamp. The door creaked and the flame flickered. He turned and saw Moon Scent come in smiling. She was beautiful in the lamplight, like the fairy mistress stepping out of a book for the scholar in an old story by P'u Sung-ling.

"Not sleeping yet, Comrade Ku?" she said. She brought a warming basket with live charcoal covered with ashes and tucked it into his bed. Before it had always been Big Aunt who brought him the basket every night. It was her idea at the beginning. He protested to no avail and afterward learned to appreciate it as the nights were very chilly. Big Aunt must have told Moon Scent just now that he required one every night. He was angry with the old woman for being so damn solicitous. Nobody around here ever made use of those baskets except the old and infirm. He did not mind it so much when Big Aunt brought it to his bed, but with Moon Scent it was different. It made him feel like such an old woman.

"This is not necessary. Really!" he murmured.

She smiled at him. "No trouble at all." And she was gone.

The basket made a big, ungainly hump at the foot of the bed. He sat down disconsolately on the bed and turned to gaze at it. He had never been so afraid of the cold as this winter. It must be due to the lack of nourishment. The light was burning low as he picked up his pen to finish his letter. Peevishly he poked at the wick with a strip of bamboo and the light went out altogether. He could not find his matchbox in the dark. It must have been put away somewhere when he was moving house.

There was nothing left to do but to go to bed. The rain drummed on. Hunger kept him awake and the thought of Moon Scent bothered him. What would she look like next summer when she could take off this ungainly padded uniform? He turned and tossed so much that he worried about upsetting the basket, scorching his blanket, and perhaps starting a fire.

Toward dawn he made a resolution. The next day, when the rain had stopped, he walked to town to mail his letter and eat in the restaurant as usual. But before he came back he bought some provisions to take home with him—a thing he had never done before. He got a quantity of dried dates and tea-leaf eggs—eggs hard-boiled with tea leaves and spices. He felt very guilty about it, since he was supposed to live with the farmers and eat what they ate.

That night, when he had eaten the eggs and the red dates, he carefully wrapped up the shells and date seeds in a piece of paper. In the morning he went out for a walk. It was funny how the country was such a large, disheveled sort of place and yet it was so difficult to dispose of garbage of this sort. He had to go far out into the hills and scatter the scraps in the long grass.

Moon Scent was washing his socks and handkerchiefs for him. In late afternoon, when they were dry, she folded them up neatly and took them to his room, perhaps meaning to stay and chat for a while. She was not above flirting with this city man a little, though she would never admit that to herself.

It was already dark in his room but the lamp was not yet lit. As she stood in the doorway, she did not at first perceive that he was munching a tea-leaf egg. When she realized it, she was as embarrassed as he was.

"Your socks are dry, Comrade Ku." She smiled at him hastily as she laid them at the foot of his bed and retreated with as natural an air as possible.

At suppertime Ku brought the two remaining eggs to the table and with some awkwardness offered to share them with the family. He bought them in town the other day and had forgotten all about them, he said. He put up such a poor performance, that he was much vexed with himself. But it was difficult to behave naturally about a thing like food when it aroused the lowest and most savage instincts in all of them and had become the object of quite indecent cravings.

Moon Scent made her refusal with a set smile. Gold Root grabbed hold of his arms to ward off the eggs. But finally they had to give in so as not to be rude. Throughout supper they talked even less than usual, although Gold Root felt that he had to comment politely. "A good egg. Yes—a good egg." And afterward there was a perceptible coldness in their attitude toward their guest.

After that Moon Scent seldom came into Ku's room. And whenever she did, she always warned him of her approach by talking loudly to someone else. This assumption that he might be eating any time of the day was outrageous and somehow humiliating.

Apparently Beckon had also been forbidden to enter his room. He never actually saw Beckon peeping at him but her mother probably caught her at it more than once. All of a sudden the air would be loud with the sound of scolding and chastisement and the child's crying.

He made frequent trips to town now, always on some pretext. He brought home dates, rock-hard sesame cakes six inches in diameter, and small sesame cakes called "gold-coin cakes"—he had eaten those before but had never noticed how terribly crunchy they were. This furtive eating with his back to the door was, he felt, a degrading experience. But it did quiet his hunger and mental turmoil so that he was able to get on with his writing.

One afternoon he was sunning his back in the courtyard working on the story of the dam. Moon Scent was sitting under the eaves doing her mending. The child stood close by her side. Ku was absorbed in his work, and it was some time before he noticed the goings on over there. The child, her face set and stubborn, was rubbing hard against her mother, so hard that Moon Scent, seemingly oblivious of her, swayed and jolted a bit with her movements. And the child mumbled under her breath and made small plaintive noises through her nose. Now and then she gave a despairing tug to her mother's jacket.

"What are you whining at?" Moon Scent suddenly exploded, thrusting her off. "What is it you want from me, you little pest? Every day like this, whether there are people around or not. Shameless! A born beggar! Every day—every day like this! I don't know what I owed you in my last life. Why don't you die? Why don't you die, you worthless little pest!"

The child burst out crying, drawing her two sleeves alternately over her streaming eyes. Moon Scent, who never left off working at her mending, went on saying the same things over and over again, without looking at the child. And then, just when it appeared as if her anger was being gradually worked off, a fresh spurt of rage took hold of her. With a deliberate movement she put down her mending. She was careful to stitch the needle on the cloth so as not to lose it. The child knew what was coming. She ran around in circles wringing her hands, gibbering with terror. Her wizened little face seemed strangely old, and there was something primeval in her exaggerated, theatrical exhibition of horror and distress. Ku looked on aghast. For a moment he even felt the impulse of instant flight, as if he himself were faced with an enemy before whose might he was utterly powerless.

The blows fell. Beckon shrieked with each slap.

"All right, all right, Sister-in-Law Gold Root!" Ku came forward and tried to separate them. "Stop it—that's enough! You can't expect the little girl to act like a grownup. Now, let her go!"

She ignored him completely. If anything, his intervention only served to goad her on. When she finally finished with the child, she returned to her mending. Beckon stood blubbering in the middle of the courtyard.

"Wipe your nose," shouted Moon Scent.

Ku went back to his seat. Presently the sun went down and he returned to his room, taking the chair with him. Moon Scent never once glanced in his direction.

The child was very quiet and timid that evening. After she went to sleep, when Moon Scent was sitting by the side of the bed doing her sewing, she felt a twinge of remorse.

She suddenly said to Gold Root, "When the New Year comes, we must buy some pork and cook something for Beckon."

So she still had money left, thought Gold Root. She did not lend it all to her mother. He despised himself for thinking that, as if he was spying on her, but he could not help it.

Then she regretted what she had said and turned around to scan the face of the sleeping child. "If she heard me there would be no end of trouble." She giggled with a guilty air. But after a while she again said musingly, "All we need is a little pork fat. With a little pork fat we can make rice-flour balls with bean-paste stuffing. Children like sweet things."

THE WOMEN'S ASSOCIATION WAS GOING TO **9** hold a meeting. As usual, Moon Scent went next door to pick up Sister-in-Law Gold Have Got.

"She is washing clothes by the stream," said Big Aunt.

After Moon Scent left, Big Aunt grumbled after her, "If you want someone to go, go yourself. No, you must drag others along. Other people have work to do. In this family the old ones are too old and the young ones too young. Who is going to do the work if she goes to meetings all day long? Calling for her all the time, like calling the soul of the dying back to the body. You still aren't the Chairman of the Women's Association. You need not be so anxious, dropping in at every house to drag other people to the meeting. Husband and wife—husband and wife certainly think alike. So you are a Labor Model." She switched over to Gold Root, her voice going higher and higher. "People just give you a few words of praise and you lose your head. You do not stop to think: where is the nine *tan* of grain you reaped? Where has it gone to? You end up just as empty-bellied as we are."

"All right, all right, say no more!" whispered Big Uncle.

"*Ai,* the young people are such fools!" Big Aunt sighed as she sat there plaiting flax. "They cannot hear a few kind words without wanting to lay down their lives for somebody. They willingly dig out their hearts and dig out their livers. I, the old woman, have lived longer than you people. Just the salt I have eaten would make a bigger pile than all the rice you have put in your bellies. The things I have seen are many. One moment this army comes; one moment that army comes. After the army come the bandits. And this time it is worse than any bandits. You can't even bury four ounces of millet underground and get away with it. Yes, they always know."

"*Hai-yah,* Old Lord Heaven, what kind of talk is this?" cried Big Uncle. "Gone crazy today!"

At this Big Aunt started to shout, "Don't be afraid, old man! Don't be afraid! I won't get you involved. Let them report me. Let them gain credits. No matter how anxious to please Comrade Wong—they still end up just as empty-bellied as we are."

Big Uncle finally gave up trying to stop her. He knew that Gold Root was in the hills gathering firewood and that Comrade Ku had gone to town to buy the food he ate in secret. They had seen Gold Root going out. But it happened that he had returned without being seen and was in his room all this time.

Moon Scent also had come back because she forgot to tell Gold Root to keep an eye on the child and see that she did not slip into Comrade Ku's room. As soon as she entered the courtyard she heard Big Aunt's voice yelling, but she could not make out whether she was quarreling with the old man or scolding her daughter-in-law. When she came to her own room, she found Gold Root standing near the doorway in a gangling, awkward pose.

She jerked her head toward next door. "Quarreling with whom?" she asked.

He looked at her uncomprehendingly.

Then she heard what Big Aunt was shouting. Gold Root's face was harsh with pain. She looked away from it quickly. She hated that old woman for hurting him.

"Big Aunt, don't talk so loudly!" she shouted across the wall. "It is all right if we hear you. But what if somebody else hears and goes to report you? You would blame it on us and we would never be able to clear ourselves."

"Don't think I am afraid of being reported!" Big Aunt shouted back. "An old woman like me is a candle in the wind and frost on the tiles—I cannot last long anyhow. But you people who are young and have a future to think of—do not blacken your heart and do harm to others or you would not come to a good end."

"All right, all right, say one sentence less," urged Big Uncle.

"Calling other people black-hearted for no reason," yelled Moon Scent. "An elder not behaving like an elder —living to a great age, but all your days seem to have been lived out by a dog."

"You dare scold me! Am I someone whom you might scold?" her aunt cried out. "Crazy! Do you eat rice or do you eat dung?"

"Everybody say one sentence less," pleaded Big Uncle.

"Let it go at that," said Gold Root to his wife.

"The dead hag!" hissed Moon Scent. "Why do you not die, you dead hag?"

"Ah, you women!" Gold Root said disgustedly.

"Go and report me! Get my daughter-in-law to report me to the Women's Association! Go ahead!"

"You never will stop—never will stop," said Big Uncle between clenched teeth, and there was a sound of scuffling and muffled blows.

"All right, beat me! Beat me!" wailed Big Aunt. "At my age, with my grandsons so big already, you still beat me? Beat me to death then! I don't want to live! I haven't the face to go on living."

Things clattered to the ground as Big Aunt rolled all over the room howling with grief.

"Go and make peace between them," said Gold Root to Moon Scent.

"I certainly am not going."

Gold Root finally went himself. "All right, all right, Big Uncle." He pulled the old man aside. "At your age, and married for so many years—people will laugh."

Big Aunt sat on the ground boo-hooing. Stray short hair, white and tough like cats' whiskers, fell over her cheeks.

Panting with his exertions, Big Uncle turned a desperately beseeching face to Gold Root and tried to explain how this madness suddenly came over her and it really had nothing to do with Moon Scent. Gold Root managed to shake him off. When he came home the room was empty. Moon Scent had gone to the meeting.

From that day onward Big Aunt and Moon Scent ceased speaking to each other.

KU HAD BEEN GOING TO THE VILLAGE PUBLIC **10**
Office every day the last few days, to help
write antithetical couplets for the Spring Scrolls to be
sold to the farmers during the New Year. Householders
always bought a new set every year to paste on the folding
doors. Prices varied with the number of words. In the
old days the wording usually went like this:

"On this ground, blessings abound and sons are born;
Within this door, gold piles up and jade accumulates."

But now it was more likely to be

"May Chairman Mao live to ten thousand years;

May the Communist Party weather a thousand autumns."

The characters were just as beautifully balanced and looked just as handsome as before in lustrous black on plain red or coral-patterned paper. But somehow it was not the same.

It was on a cold, dark, snow-brewing day that Gold Root's sister Gold Flower came home from Chou Village. Ku was still home when she came, so she and her family just sat around chatting without saying much. As soon as Ku left, she started telling her family about her troubles. Her mother-in-law, she said, was more polite to her than to the others because she was a newcomer. So her sisters-in-law could not stand it and banded up together to say bad things about her. They said she was lazy and greedy and her husband starved himself to save his food for her. Her mother-in-law believed this and got very angry and scolded the son. It was all lies, Gold Flower said, though it was a fact that they all were not eating much.

When Moon Scent returned from Shanghai and brought her back presents, the towel and the scented soap, it had caused a lot of comment. Ever since then Gold Flower's new in-laws had always been hinting that she should go back home and borrow money. This time her mother-in-law openly asked her to do it, saying that otherwise they could not possibly get through the New Year.

"Ai-yah," said Moon Scent, "if I had only known how hard up we are in the country, I would never have bought those things and made trouble for you."

Gold Flower went on recounting her sufferings in a stolid monotone, her eyes fixed on the ground and her hands tucked under her jacket. The room was very cold.

There were pauses in which they all sat breathing out white smoke.

"Be patient, Sister," Moon Scent consoled her. "You are fortunate that Brother-in-Law treats you well. Although life is hard for the time being, it cannot be helped. It is the same with everybody. As to what kind of a life we lead here at home, other people may not know how it is, but you know, Sister." In turn she began a detailed account of how bad things were in their own household.

Gold Root listened and said nothing. He could not expect his wife to part with what little was left of her savings. But his bowels turned with anguish when he thought of the time when he and his sister were children together. Whenever he caught a good cricket he gave it to her. And on the third of the third moon when the townfolk came out to the country to visit their ancestral graves, he ran from grave to grave and hovered around waiting for the give-away rice-flour balls. He was very good at collecting those cakes so that there was always plenty for both of them.

In summer he caught grasshoppers in the fields, tied them up with a blade of grass, and asked his mother to fry them in oil, the whole string of them, till they were half-burned and crisp and tasty.

They had always been poor. He remembered lying in bed in the morning when his mother was taking rice out of the great earthen jar, and he could hear the dipper scrape against the bottom of the jar. At that dreaded scratchy sound he felt a chilly, acidy sadness seep into his bones.

And one day he knew there was nothing to eat in the house. As lunchtime approached he called out to his sister, "Come out and play, Sister Gold Flower." Gold Flower, being much younger than he, had no sense of time. They played and played in the fields. Then he heard his mother calling them, "Gold Root! Gold Flower! Come have your lunch!" He was astonished. They went home and he found she had boiled some beans which she had meant to keep for seeds. The beans were very nice. His mother sat watching them with a smile as they ate.

Now he was fully grown and an owner of land, and yet it seemed he was just as helpless as before against the force of circumstances. His sister came to him weeping and he had to send her away empty-handed.

Sitting with knees wide apart, he bent forward until he was almost doubled up, one hand fumbling around with the back of his neck. When Gold Flower's long story was at an end, Moon Scent rose and went over to the other side to prepare lunch.

Then he also got up and walked over to Moon Scent who was taking rice out of the great earthen jar.

"I want to have a meal of properly cooked rice today, instead of that watery stuff," he said in a low voice. "I want it hard enough for the grains to be counted."

"All right. Now go away. It would look queer to Sister," she mumbled under her breath without turning her head.

When he came back to Gold Flower, she had dried her tears and was playing with Beckon. Leading the child by the hand, she peeped into Ku's room.

"Let me have a look at my old room," she said.

"You must not go inside," said Beckon, "or Ma will beat you."

"Why?"

"And you must not look in when the man is at home. He will be eating and Ma would beat you."

Beckon enjoyed romping around with her aunt. Then it was time for lunch. They had the same thin gruel as they had always, with some stringy wild vegetables floating in it. Gold Root was so angry he could hardly get it down his throat. He ate in silence, then suddenly set down his bowl with a clatter and went outside the house to smoke his pipe.

It began to snow. At first the tiny flakes were only visible against the dark bulk of the hill. Then they could be seen as myriads of grayish specks descending slowly from the white sky. Gold Flower said she had to start back. Moon Scent asked her to wait and see if the snow would stop, but she seemed restless. After a while she again stood up to go.

"Do not go, Aunt. Stay with us." Beckon hung on to her.

Moon Scent said jokingly, "If you don't let her go back home to your new uncle, he'll come and beat you up."

Gold Root took his huge orange oilpaper umbrella and thrust it into his sister's hand.

"But you might need it yourself," Gold Flower protested, not looking at him but at her sister-in-law.

Moon Scent assured her they could easily drop in and fetch it someday when they passed by Chou Village. They saw her out to the road, the two women walking under the umbrella, with Gold Root following a few steps behind. But before they reached the mouth of the village he turned back abruptly without a word of farewell.

The snow soon turned into rain, as it often did here, south of the Yangtze. Moon Scent came home alone without an umbrella. She was wiping her clothes when Gold Root went at her.

"I told you not to give us that thin gruel for lunch. I

would have thrown it in your face if Sister hadn't been here."

"We ate what we always ate. Sister is no guest."

"She seldom ever comes and you even grudge her a full meal."

"If we cook something special for her she would think that is what we have every day. She would think we are well off and yet we still won't lend her money."

Gold Root said, after pausing for reflection, "She would never think that of us."

"She is just a child. Besides, she would tell her husband, and the whole family would know. You know how people talk."

"She need not tell anybody."

"I would have told you, if it had been me!"

He was silent after that.

The room was dark and close in the rainy afternoon, with a smell of wet cloth shoes. Gold Root went and lay down on the bed. After some time he sat up with a jerk, rolled up the old, much-patched wadded blanket, slung it over one shoulder, and started for the door.

"What are you doing?" cried Moon Scent. "Where are you going?"

"I am going to pawn this and buy me a drink of wine."

"You are crazy!" She clutched at the blanket with all her strength. "We would freeze to death in this weather."

"What do I care? This kind of life is not worth living."

"Who ever heard of anything like this—pawn the wadded blanket in the middle of 'the nine's'![1] We would die of cold!"

"I'll try and get into a game of dominoes; with my winnings I can redeem it."

[1] The Chinese divide winter into nine times nine days.

"No, no!" she gasped.

She tugged and he tugged, and she began to weep out of exasperation. Suddenly he let go and turned away disgusted. She flopped down hard on the dirt floor. Then she picked herself up, and the blanket and, still crying, shook the dust off it.

"But what did he expect me to do?" she thought. "Lend her money to help feed all her in-laws while we starve to death?"

She had to keep telling herself that, to whet her anger. Because even though she had all the reasons on her side she felt unaccountably guilty. He seemed so depressed that it alarmed her.

After supper she went to bed early, rolling the blanket tightly around Beckon and herself. Later, when Gold Root came to bed and tried to pull the blanket loose, she held on firmly and said, "You can do without the blanket. You are not afraid of the cold."

He gave the blanket such a jerk that it nearly landed her and the child on the floor. Then, to her surprise, he blew out the lamp and lay down quietly with all his clothes on. He did not seem to care one way or the other.

He lay awake for a long time. He wanted very much to take her in his arms and drown his sorrows in her, in place of the drink that was denied him. But he was deeply ashamed of himself. And in China the commonest joke is that about the poor man who, though starving, is still amorous, and is jeered at by his wife.

Near midnight, when she was sure he was asleep, she spread out the blanket and, feeling around in the dark, tucked it in under him. And in his sleep his arms slid around her out of habit.

A RESOLUTION HAD BEEN PASSED BY THE **11** Farmers' Association that during the New Year the villagers would visit the Soldiers' Families in the neighborhood to wish them a happy New Year and send them gifts. Each household would contribute half a pig and forty catties of New Year cakes. All contributors were supposed to drape the presents with red and green streamers and deliver them at the proper doors with the Rice-Sprout Song Corps dancing and making music. A slip of red paper with the words "Glorious Family" written on it would be pasted over the doors of lucky families with sons in service, amid the explosion of firecrackers.

Households who owned no pig would pay money instead and everybody was asked to pay a certain sum for the firecrackers. All contributions were to be delivered to the Village Public Office by the twenty-fifth of the twelfth moon. But the day passed without anybody making a move. The farmers had unanimously raised their hands in favor of the proposition without quite knowing how they were to fulfill it. So each man waited to see what his neighbors were going to do about it.

The Chairman of the Farmers' Association and his wife, who was the Chairman of the Women's Association, called meetings and talked to each family separately without getting any results. Comrade Wong had to visit every house in turn to put pressure on the peasants. At Gold Root's house he said, "Gold Root T'an, you are a Labor Model and a Positive Element in the village. You ought to set an example for others. We must carry out this task. It is really a political task, with political significance. Doesn't that mean anything to you? The families of soldiers in the People's Liberation Army ought to be taken care of. Without the People's Liberation Army how would you have got your land? In the old days the soldiers did nothing except bring trouble to the people. Now it is different. Now the army is the people's own army. And the people and the soldiers are supposed to be one family."

Gold Root still argued that he could not produce the money or the rice for New Year cakes. "Why, we have eaten rice gruel for the last two months," he said.

Alarmed by his curtness, Moon Scent hurriedly cut in with a gently sad but lengthy account of all their hardships and privations.

"Every family has its troubles," Wong said, smiling. "But look at the other villages. They are no better off than we are. And yet they buy New Year presents for Soldiers' Families just the same. Are we any less patriotic than the others?" He stepped one foot on the bench, composing himself for a long, cozy chat.

When Gold Root insisted for a third time that he had neither rice nor money, he said with a grin, "I know you are not having an easy time. But at least it is not so bad with you people as with some of the others. Your wife had been working in the city. Both of you produce, and you have very few people in your family. You have always eaten better than the others, for one thing."

Gold Root flushed darkly. Of course Comrade Wong was referring to that time when he caught them eating rice gruel thicker than what people usually had, on Moon Scent's first day home. Gold Root knew it was all his own fault, which enraged him all the more, and he lost control of himself. "Comrade Wong," he shouted, "you ask around here! People will tell you what we eat every day—who can hide anything from anybody else? As it is, our rice is running out. Here the New Year is upon us and my heart feels as if it is being fried in oil."

Moon Scent went frantic in her efforts to stop him. But Comrade Wong kept a smile fixed on his face and continued to reason with him. This was the kind of thing Wong could do in his sleep. He carried on for hours and could have gone on forever, since they were arguing on parallel lines. Gold Root insisted on his destitution. And Wong, not believing him, harangued him on his duty to the Soldiers' Families.

"Do not make your troubles look bigger than they are. Look farther ahead, Comrade," he counseled.

"But how can we, when we won't have anything to eat next spring? Are we going to have 'big pot rice'?"

Comrade Wong was rattled for the first time at the mention of "big pot rice." Before Liberation, Nationalist agents had tried to frighten the peasants by telling them the Communists were going to force them to pool their food stocks and eat from a single kitchen. The peasants had always dreaded the idea of a communal "big pot" for all. By now, though, they had come to the state where they were fervently wishing for it, thinking of it as a form of government relief.

"You people would fare much better if you stop dreaming about 'big pot rice' and try to get more out of your own land," snapped Comrade Wong. With his smile gone it looked as if a regular feature were missing from his face. It was frightening.

"Do not listen to him, Comrade Wong," babbled Moon Scent. "He is grouchy today because yesterday I kept him from pawning our wadded blanket and going on a spree."

They both ignored her. "After the spring famine will come the summer famine! And then where will we be?" yelled Gold Root.

Wong pounded the table. "This attitude of yours is very wrong, Gold Root T'an. I have been patient with you because of your past efforts. But don't go too far. What has come over you? Is anybody 'holding on to your hind legs'?"

He was, of course, referring to Moon Scent, who had stolen away while they were talking. She had fled to the dark recesses at the side of the bed from which she presently emerged holding something in her hand. Flushed with inner struggle, she approached Wong and said with a steady smile, "Comrade Wong, I have some money here which he knows nothing about. It is all I have left.

Please take it and buy firecrackers for us. And we want to pay for half a pig to give as a present to the Soldiers' Families. I've never told him I have this money."

Comrade Wong went on pounding the table and shouting at Gold Root as if he had not heard her, keeping her waiting for what seemed to be a long time. Gold Root glared at her as if he would strike her dead on the spot.

At last Wong turned to her and said icily, "Why did you not say so before? All this talk about being penniless —playing such a rascally trick with your own government!"

"Yes, I was wrong, Comrade Wong. But he really did not know I had the money. He knew nothing."

"See that the New Year cakes are ready by the day after tomorrow—time is short. And talk to him and straighten out his way of thinking. His attitude today is very wrong."

Moon Scent saw Comrade Wong out of the courtyard and waited respectfully in the doorway until he disappeared into another house. Suddenly she felt her hair grabbed from behind. Gold Root slapped her right and left and she kicked and fought back wildly. She did not scream—in case Wong was not yet out of earshot.

But Gold Root would not keep quiet. "So you have money!" he said. "And you throw it about. Who wants your stinking money? So you make me look like a liar! I'll teach you to make me out a liar!"

In spite of herself she let out a yelp under the impact of the blows. Big Uncle came, and so did Big Aunt, though she had not been on speaking terms with Moon Scent ever since they quarreled and the old man gave her a beating. The old woman came to intervene because she was warmhearted and always on the spot whenever there was trouble. Besides, it was pleasant to watch an adversary being humiliated, even as she herself had been humiliated before all.

"Now, now, Gold Root," said Big Uncle. "There is nothing that cannot be talked over peaceably. Gentlemen move their lips; rascals move their hands."

"All right, enough now, Gold Root! Comrade Wong might hear you," Big Aunt said tactlessly, or perhaps on purpose.

"Do not frighten me with Comrade Wong," said Gold Root, hitting harder. "And she can go and report to the Women's Association. I am not afraid!"

The old couple finally managed to tear them apart and Gold Root stamped out of the courtyard.

"The one thing wrong with Gold Root is his temper," said Big Aunt. "That's what I have always said. He should not have wasted his anger on his wife."

Moon Scent said nothing. When Big Aunt helped her into her room, she threw herself face downward on the bed and abandoned herself to stifling sobs.

Big Aunt sat down on the bed. "Fighting between married couples is a common thing. Do not take him seriously. Haven't you heard the saying, 'Between husband and wife there is no grudge that lasts overnight'?" Then bending over Moon Scent she whispered, "You are not the only family who suffers. With us it is worse. Our pig is done for. We cannot produce the money, so we are told to borrow from relatives. 'Doesn't your daughter-in-law have a sister who married a shopkeeper in town?'—the turtle's egg knows everything. Now she has gone to town to see her sister. I do not know what would happen if they should refuse to lend the money." She sighed and bent down to wipe her eyes on the skirt of her jacket. "*Ai,* not easy!—to pass from one day to another."

Moon Scent went on weeping convulsively. To her the sky had blacked out and she was choked with earth and buried alive under a mountain, because Gold Root did not understand her.

On the following day they began at dawn to grind the rice into flour to make New Year cakes. The creak of the old millstone was heavy and painfully slow. It was the sound of the earth turning on its axis, the passage of long months and years.

In the evening they moved a table into the courtyard and, placing a candle in the center of the table, stood around it still making New Year cakes. With both hands Gold Root deftly kneaded a big white ball of rice flour, the size of a watermelon and burning hot. Bending over the table, he kept rolling it very fast, with a curious little smile on his lips and the intense concentration of one who was fashioning something out of burning rock at the beginning of the world. From time to time he would pluck off a small piece and toss it to Moon Scent, who would press it into a small wooden mold, then empty the mold by knocking it on the table. A tiny brush made of five goose feathers tied together stood in a tin full of rouge water. She would mark the cake three times with the brush, making three red plum blossoms, blurrily superimposed on the embossed design of orchids and plum blossoms. Beckon noisily insisted that she could make those marks, but the table was too high for her.

At last the cakes were done and removed to the room where they were stacked up to dry. There was a lot of counting to be done, and calculating whether they came

122

up to the required weight. In the deserted courtyard the candle still glowed at the center of the table, which was bare except for the tin can in which a piece of "cotton-wool rouge" was soaked in water.

Moon Scent came over, fished out the piece of dripping cotton wool, and rubbed it at random over her cheeks and eyelids, then smoothed over the redness with her palms.

"No sense in wasting it," she said with a short laugh. She called for the child and also applied it to her face. For the rest of the evening the mother and daughter went about with their cheeks a flaming, theatrical red. It did look as if the New Year was here.

12

EVEN BEFORE THE SUN WAS UP SOME OF THE pigs in the village had already gone to their deaths in honor of the Glorious Soldiers' Families. From a distance their shrill, hoarse cries sounded like desperate long blasts on a rusty whistle.

In midmorning Big Uncle turned his own pig loose in the compound—an unpaved, sunken square in the middle of the village, with stone steps leading up to the surrounding houses. Long gray stains of various shades streaked the white walls of the houses—the cheerless water color done by rain.

"Don't kill the pig out there," fussed Big Aunt. "Do it in our own courtyard. Outside, with lots of people watching, somebody might say something that is not auspicious. Have to be careful, with the New Year so near."

"It does not matter. This time we are not doing it for ourselves," Big Uncle said wearily. "If we do it properly we will have to light the incense and candles and then kill it, since this is only a few days before the New Year."

The pig had already been starved for a whole day to cleanse its stomach. It nosed eagerly around on the bare, pale brown earth of winter, searching for edibles. Suddenly it uttered a loud cry—one of Big Uncle's neighbors had grabbed it by its hind legs. Somebody else came to help drag it, and presently it was turned on its back, lying on a raised wooden frame. Big Aunt held its front and hind legs while Big Uncle bent down to reach for his knife from his basketful of instruments. But first he removed his long pipe from his mouth and thrust it through the end of the basket handle. The basket was beautiful with a surplus length of bamboo split which the weaver had not bothered to cut off and so it was left to sprout forth from one side with the long, graceful sweep of an orchid leaf in a Chinese painting.

The pig went right on calling out with undiminished volume long after the pointed knife had been plunged into its throat. And the sound never changed—always a flat, expressionless, grating cry, uglier than the horse's neigh. But it was considered bad luck when the pig screamed too much, so toward the end Big Uncle put out a hand to hold its mouth. After a while it made a low grunt as if saying: No use arguing with these people. And it became silent.

White steam continued to issue from its snout. The weather was very cold.

The old man had wrapped flaxen bags on his legs to

keep warm. A dog of the same shade of pale yellow as his leggings came and lapped up the blood that streamed down to the ground from the pig's throat. Then it nosed around the place, hoping to find more of it. Lifting its head, it happened to knock against the pig's leg, stretched out stiffly in the air. It smelled the leg curiously. Whatever conclusion it reached was obviously to its satisfaction. It trotted around, ducking now and then under the pig's legs, an unmistakably smiling expression in its shining black eyes.

Sister-in-law Gold Have Got came with a flat-pole on her shoulder, carrying two buckets of hot water which she poured into a big wooden tub. They lowered the pig into the tub, forcibly pressing its head into the water. When the head emerged again into view, the black hair was all messed up and fluffy like that of a child taking a bath. Big Uncle picked its ears with an ear spoon, for the first time in its experience. Then he shaved the body with a big razor that furled inward at both ends. Big balls of hair fell off at each deft stroke. Then, digging a little pick into the hoof, he removed the claws one by one with great ease. The little snow-white ankle ending in a tiny pink sole looked as if it belonged to a woman with bound feet, where the toes were all bunched together.

The old man had to blow from the hoof to inflate the pig. That would make it easier to pluck off the hairs. He had done this countless times in his life, and yet he hesitated a little, as he always did, before inserting the hoof into his mouth.

A circle of spectators had collected around the scene. The few comments they made were confined to estimates of how many catties this pig weighed as compared to the weight of some other family's pig killed yesterday and the record-making weight of another family's pig slaughtered last year.

"This pig is only fat in the front quarters," said a tall, cadaverous old man with square, high shoulders, wearing a long gray gown.

Nobody said anything to that. All their remarks were monologues.

The tall old man went back to his own house and soon turned up again with a blue-rimmed bowl and a pair of chopsticks and ate up his bowl of steaming gruel as he stood there looking on.

Sister-in-Law Gold Have Got came with a kettle of boiling water and poured it on the pig. Finally all the hairs were removed except for a patch on the head. Made to sprawl over the side of the tub, face downward, the pig now looked alarmingly human, the plump white form bald except for this black patch at the back of the head. And when at last Big Uncle and Big Aunt hoisted the carcass around and the hairless porcine face came into view, it was a laughing face, the merry little eyes squeezed into curved slits.

Later the carcass was brought indoors and laid on a table, refrigerated by the intense cold of the end of the Lunar Year. The head had been cut off. The big white snout rested contentedly on the table. Following tradition —a tradition that showed a somewhat grotesque sense of fun—they made the slain pig hold its curly little tail in its mouth with a playful, kittenish air.

Their pigsty also served as a privy, as was usual in the village. Tall wooden pails stood precariously on the border of the pit in which the pig used to be kept. In the afternoon, when the old man went to empty the urine pails, he glanced briefly into the darkness. The room seemed very silent without the familiar grunts and vague stirrings of the recumbent form in the pit.

He felt shaken and spent as he walked out of the empty sty into the thin yellow sunshine. His daughter-in-law was in the courtyard scrubbing grease off the wooden tub. His wife was sitting on the doorsill wiping his butchering tools with a piece of rag before putting them away in the basket. He went and stood under the eaves, his hands thrust under his blue work skirt, tucking it up.

"I will never rear a pig again," he said aloud.

"You have said that before," said the old woman. Seeing that he made no remark to that, she added with a cruel insistence, "That was what you said the other time."

"Whoever rears a pig again is the son of a bitch," he said in a loud voice, not looking at her.

Sister-in-Law Gold Have Got had begun to cry. Her hands being greasy, she just raised a shoulder and wiped her eyes on the upper part of the sleeve. Warm tears streamed down her face and the wind quickly fanned them cold.

All three of them were thinking of "the other time." That was years ago, during the Japanese occupation.

The house they lived in had been built by the only branch of the family that had prospered and produced mandarins. The dilapidated white mansion that now housed a clan of small farmers still proclaimed in a gilded signboard over the front gate, "Residence of a *Ching Sse*," a *ching sse* being one who had passed the highest imperial examination. The signboard had been removed after the Communists came, but during the war it was still there.

The innumerable courtyards were connected by stone-paved dark passages that were more like alleys, though they were roofed in. Hawkers were free to come and go through the house, peddling their wares along those passages. And a blind beggar might wander into the house, his bamboo stick tapping a crisp, clear "tick tick" on the stone pavement. This other time, too, it was near the end of the year, like now. The blind man had chanted loudly a jingle full of auspicious sayings, wishing the housewives good luck in the coming year:

" . . . EVERY STEP SAFE, AND EVERY STEP A RAISE,
FOR YOU LADIES WHO'RE MAKING NEW YEAR CAKES . . ."

After him came a hawker of sesame oil, with two earthen jars dangling from a flat-pole on his shoulder, calling out "*Shiang yiu yao ba—shiang yiu?* Fragrant oil —want fragrant oil?"

After the hawker passed, the stillness of the afternoon fell upon the house and the village around it. Big Aunt had been alone in the courtyard grinding maize. Standing in the shadows, now and then she would put out a hand into the sunlight, smoothing the layer of corn over the grindstone. The golden corn flour descended in a sluggish stream, a slow cascade of desert sand.

She suddenly raised her head, listening hard at a faint tap-tap along the passage. It was not the blind man's stick but leather soles striking against the stone pavement. There were soldiers of the *Ho Ping Kuan*, the Peace Army of the puppet government, stationed at the Temple of the Militant Sage, and they often came into the village.

Even as she was listening, somebody crashed through their back door that led into the passage and she heard loud, excited voices in the room behind her.

"Let me stay here for a while," gasped the hawker of sesame oil. "They are coming! I saw them coming!"

"No use your hiding here, if they are coming this way," said Big Uncle.

"Let me out then, through the other door." The hawker rushed into the courtyard, banging his oil jars against the door.

"Careful, careful!" said Big Uncle.

"They are coming!" Big Aunt whispered stupidly to her husband. Then she dashed out of the gate and stooped to pick up the balls of freshly made rice-flour noodles which were set out to dry in the sun, like little nests of straw on the ground.

"Never mind those." The old man came panting after her. "Come and help me with the pig."

"I know just where to hide it," Big Aunt whispered excitedly. "Take it into the room."

They both rushed to the pigsty. The big fat sow was a wriggly, unwieldly weight in the old man's arms as he tried to lift her. Sister-in-Law Gold Have Got, who was breast-feeding a baby, bustled in and, passing the child to the old woman, stooped down to lend a helping hand.

Big Aunt stamped her feet at her daughter-in-law. "What are you doing here? Run off and hide yourself—hurry!"

"Ai, quick, quick! Hide yourself!" With horror the old man looked up at her from the ground.

"Here, you forgot the baby," Big Aunt cried out with annoyance, running after her daughter-in-law and thrusting the child into her arms.

Seeing her reminded the old man of her husband. "Hey, where is Gold Have Got?" he shouted. "He mustn't be seen. The soldiers will tie him up and take him away for a recruit!"

"*Ai*, tell him to hide himself, quick," quavered the old woman. "Here, let me have the baby, stupid! You want him to burst out crying, and ruin you?"

She propped the baby up against the wall and went back to help the old man with the pig. The two of them managed to move the animal into their living quarters. Even under those circumstances they felt a fleeting thrill of pride at the great weight it had achieved.

"The bed," gasped Big Aunt. "Put it on the bed and cover it up."

Grunting protests, the sow was dumped on the bed and covered with an old padded blanket of bright red cotton with little white flowers. The old woman drew the blanket over its head and tucked it in all round. For the finishing touch she bent down and fished under the bed for a pair of shoes, placing them in front of the bed.

They could already hear voices at the gate.

"You didn't bolt the door, did you?" she asked anxiously. "No use bolting the door—it will only make them angry."

The soldiers had already stomped in, heralded by the agitated hen they were chasing.

"Hey, nobody home?" one of them shouted. "Everybody dead in this house?"

The old couple hurried forth, smiling welcome. There were three of them, all from the north, speaking a dialect that was hard to grasp.

"Huh—pretending to be deaf," they said impatiently.

Finally it was made clear that they were asking if there was anything to eat in the house. The old woman started on her familiar tale of poor harvest and starvation. Meanwhile, one soldier, the one whose face was badly pocked with the scars of smallpox, had been doing some individual exploring over the other side of the courtyard. A slip of yellow paper pasted on a doorframe announced a recent death in the family. Gold Root's mother had just died about a month ago. The unpainted coffin was still in the room, the body sealed inside waiting to be buried after the mourning was over. The orphans, Gold Root and Gold Flower, happened to be out in the hills digging for bamboo shoots. The pockmarked soldier walked into their room and saw the coffin. Spitting on the ground to safeguard himself against the bad luck thus incurred, he turned and went into the next room, which was Big Uncle's pigsty.

"Hey, old man, where is your pig?" he called out from inside.

"I have sold it, Captain," said the old man.

"Nonsense! How can the place be so filthy without a pig?" said the soldier, who had been a farmer before he joined up.

"These country people are real scoundrels. Full of lies," said one of them, who was much older than the rest, hollow-cheeked and sallow, with tired, hooded eyes that had faded to a pale brown. Turning those eyes on the old man, he said loudly, 'Where is the pig? Hrrmph?" This last was a savage grunt that seemed to come from a foreigner who did not speak the language. He found that very effective sometimes.

The old man quailed visibly, but the old woman came to his aid, all smiles. "Captain, the pig has really been sold. Not yet big enough to fetch a good price, but we could not hold out any longer. We need rice. *Ai-yah*, I cried when we took it to the market. We country people are really pitiful, Captains!"

"Listen to her!" The veteran smiled wearily.

His companion, a ruddy-faced boy holding a hen under each arm, stepped up threateningly to the old man. "Speak up!" he shouted, lifting the butt of his rifle. Instantly the air was loud with the flapping of wings and excited squawking. One of the hens had escaped and had run indoors, sailing over the high doorsill. The ground was strewn with feathers.

"——its grandmother!" cursed the young soldier, laughing and chasing after it. The hen flew on top of a table, and bowls and bottles fell crashing to the floor.

The others strolled in after him and stood around guffawing, leaning on their rifles as he struggled with the hen.

"Twist its neck," counseled the pockmarked one. "Make sure it is dead, if you don't want your uniform dirtied by droppings."

The veteran lifted the padded blue curtain at the door, peering into the inner room. The old woman immediately placed herself at his elbow, pleading with a smile, "We have a sick person at home, Captain. That room is filthy. Come and sit over here, Captain, sit over here."

Ignoring her words, the soldier walked in with the other two at his heels. The old woman followed them into the room, babbling, "Very sick. High fever. Mustn't be exposed to cold air. It will be fatal to catch cold at this stage." A fleeting glance at the bed reassured her that everything was just as she had left it.

The men walked around the room fingering this and that.

"Well, look around, look around," the old woman said, smiling helplessly. "There is nothing to see in a poor man's house." No sooner were the words out of her mouth when she was horrified to discover that the blanket had started to heave. The pig was growing restive.

133

Big Aunt went quickly to the head of the bed and clutched at the blanket, drawing it firmly over the great snout coming out for air. "You fool, you want to catch cold and die?" she scolded. "Now be good. Cover up your head and let yourself perspire all over, so you will get well quick. Have patience. Don't you dare let the cold air touch you before the perspiration has dried thoroughly. You hear?"

She tucked the blanket tightly around it, and, surprisingly enough, the pig stopped moving.

The veteran's experienced eyes swept over the room, looking for signs of newly turned earth on the dirt floor or patches on the mud wall which spoke of hidden treasures. The other two, failing to find anything of interest, were already arguing over ways of cooking the hens.

"Stew one and boil one," said the young soldier.

"They are too old to taste good in a stew," said the pockmarked one.

Big Aunt's heart stood still as the veteran walked up to the bed. He bent down and looked under the bed for trunks or suspicious patches on the earthen floor. Then he straightened up and was turning to go when the shoes in front of the bed happened to catch his eyes. They were homemade blue cloth shoes with a strap starting at the back of the ankle. They must belong to a young woman —they were much too large for old women with bound feet.

Big Aunt went all hollow inside with the feeling of imminent doom when she saw the sudden gleam come into his eyes.

"Hey, Pockmark!" he called out, laughing, "we have a *hua ku niung* here, a flowerlike maid!"

The pockmarked one rushed to the bed and whisked

off the blanket. After the first moment of incredulous silence they all burst into laughter and profanity.

"——his mother," cried Pockmark, "how did they ever think of such a thing! Hiding a pig in bed!"

The veteran went after the old woman, threatening her with the butt of his rifle. "You dare cheat your father, eh? Tired of living, aren't you?"

The squealing pig had hurled itself on the ground and was making for the door. In the act of grabbing its hind legs the young soldier had to let go of both his hens, which circled around the room clucking frantically, adding to the furor.

"Come and help me, somebody," shouted the boy. "Don't just stand there. Hey—block off the door!"

Pockmark helped him to catch the pig. Presently the boy found that he was carrying it on his back and it was too heavy for him. As he staggered to his feet, Pockmark jumped up and down, laughing and slapping his thighs.

"Hey, look, look!" he yelled. "Win Victory Li is coming with his mother on his back!"

Flushed with annoyance, Win Victory Li loosened his hold on the pig so that it slid down his back, dropping to the ground with a terrific thud. And he threw himself on Pockmark, grappling with him. It was the veteran's turn to catch the pig.

"Don't stand there pretending to be dead, old woman," he called out in exasperation. "Get a rope and tie it up. And sling it on a flat-pole. Otherwise how do you expect us to carry it? Such a filthy thing."

The old couple found a rope and tied up the pig. Meanwhile Pockmark, having shaken off the young boy, had picked up one of the shoes in front of the bed.

"Where is this person?" he asked the old woman.

"Now don't tell me those are your shoes. One more lie out of you and I'll beat you to death."

"Yes, where is the *hua ku niung*?" said the veteran with renewed interest.

"It's no *hua ku niung*, it's only my daughter-in-law, and she has gone home to see her mother in Peach Creek Village."

"Lying again!" Pockmark slapped her hard on the face with the sole of the shoe. He kept at it. "You old addled egg! Never a word of truth. If your father doesn't beat you to death today, I'll be surprised!"

"Don't be angry, Captain," the old woman called out, smiling, with one cheek red with the slapping. "But she is not here. I cannot produce her like a magician. Thunder strike me dead if I am not telling the truth!"

"I'll do it for him," Pockmark promised grimly.

Win Victory Li and the veteran turned on the old man. Although they slapped him and waved their bayonets at his face he also stuck to the story that their daughter-in-law was visiting with her mother.

"Let's go and look for her ourselves," said Pockmark.

"And if we find her here," the veteran warned the old couple, "don't expect to live."

The old man smiled and the old woman laughed, protesting that they had nothing to worry about, since it was a fact that their daughter-in-law was twenty *li* away, in Peach Creek Village.

"All right then, don't run away." They made the old couple accompany them as they searched the house, through deserted courtyards and rooms vacated in a hurry. They came to a haystack. The veteran thrust his bayonet into the hay, making several stabs at it. He thought he heard a half-stifled moan.

"*Ai*, the *hua ku niung* is here," he said, smiling.

"All right, let's pull the hay down. Don't stab at it any more," Pockmark said hastily, "you'll kill her."

"Don't worry," said the veteran. "Look at him! His heart is aching already because she is hurt. Crazy about her, sight unseen."

Pockmark gave him a shove that nearly threw him off balance.

"Come out," shouted the veteran. "Come out at once, or we are going to shoot."

The old couple watched in silence as a trouser leg emerged from the hay, then another. Their first feeling was of relief when they saw it was their son Gold Have Got who leaped to the ground.

"Who is this?" Pockmark cried out with disappointment.

"Your son?" asked the veteran.

"Yes, Captain," said the old woman.

"Take him with us, Win Victory Li," said the veteran. "He can carry the pig."

"No, no, kindhearted Captains," shouted Big Aunt. "He is the only son we have. His father is eighty and I am eighty-one. Who is going to see us off when we die if you take him away?" She broke down crying, falling to her knees and tugging at their legs, and she turned to tell her husband to do the same. "Beg them. They are kindhearted and generous. They will take pity on us."

Win Victory Li pointed his bayonet at Gold Have Got's back, making him march before him into the house to collect the pig. Gold Have Got was of medium height and frail like his father. He stopped once, stooping a little and laying a hand on his left shoulder where there was a spreading red stain on his clothes.

137

"Pretending to be dead," said Win Victory Li, giving him a kick. "Let it go—we'll patch you up when we get back to camp."

The old couple's last glimpse of their son was of his narrow back retreating down the road. The pig, its four feet all tied together, dangled ball-like from the flat-pole on his shoulder. The other end of the rope looped up his arm and was held by Win Victory Li. In the light of the setting sun they could see even from a distance the bits of straw sticking to his clothes.

Pockmark refused to leave until he had found the woman.

"She must be around somewhere," he said.

"Come on!" the veteran said. "If you don't hurry up and trail along, you have seen the last of that pig. Once it gets to the barracks, the sergeant will want his share; the lieutenant will want his share; the cook will keep the best portions for his cronies and his mistress. You'll be lucky to get some of the blood to boil bean curd with."

Pockmark grunted and they went off together.

Two days after they had taken the pig and the son, the platoon pulled out of the village before dawn. Other units came and went. And some of the men taken away by the soldiers managed to escape and found their way back to their home village. Big Uncle's family hoped all the time that Gold Have Got would do the same. Then one morning they heard the soldiers drilling in a clearing outside the village. There came a pause in the drills, and in the silence a broad, long, raucous howl broke out. Several well-spaced howls with silence in between. Afterward it was whispered in the village that those were deserters being punished by having their ears cut off. There were big splotches of blood in the clearing.

People could not help smiling as they passed the story around. There was something funny in the idea of having one's ears cut off. But it was not funny to Big Uncle's family. They could feel at once a whiff of cold wind blowing past their ears, leaving two bleeding holes. Big Aunt had a dream in which her son came home with his hands over his ears and she could not coax him to take off his hands and let her treat the wounds. He had always been stubborn as a child. And in her dream she was trying hard to figure out a way of saving money to buy one of those fur caps with ear flaps on them, as if that would solve his problem. She cried and cried after she woke up.

They had told the story to others, but seldom in its entirety, for fear that it would cast doubts on the chastity of their daughter-in-law. People might have a sneaking suspicion that the soldiers did find her, after all, and that the family were just saying they never found her, to save face.

As time went on and it became apparent that Gold Have Got was probably never coming back, his mother became very touchy on the subject, flying into a rage whenever anybody dared hint that he must be dead. And now, seven years later and another pig gone, she shouted at her daughter-in-law who was bending over the wooden tub in the courtyard, blubbering chokingly in the wind.

"What are you weeping for, all of a sudden?" she demanded. "With the New Year so near, it is bad luck to have all this weeping in the house. Your father-in-law and I are old but not dead yet. Wait till we are dead, then you can weep all you want."

But for once Sister-in-law Gold Have Got took no notice of her whatsoever and abandoned herself to her grief.

At length the old woman shouted in exasperation, "Stop it. Even if he is not dead, your weeping will be a curse to him and he will die. You want him to die so you can marry somebody else?"

Heartbroken at the injustice of the accusation, Sister-in-Law Gold Have Got sobbed louder than ever.

Suddenly the old woman also broke down and wept, calling out, "My hardhearted son! So many years, and never even a letter home! The hardhearted child! If you don't come back soon you will never see me again. How many more years can I wait for you?"

"All right, say no more," said the old man. "Comrade Ku is at home today," he reminded her in a whisper.

"What are you afraid of? It was the *Ho Ping Kuan* who did this to us. The *Ho Ping Kuan* dragged him off."

"Well, lots of *Ho Ping Kuan* were taken into the Nationalist Army when the war ended. If he is still alive he might be fighting for the other side."

For a moment Big Aunt was struck dumb with fear. That would make them a Counterrevolutionist Family. But she soon rallied and said brazenly, "Who knows? He might have been captured by the Communists and have become a soldier in the Liberation Army. That will make us a Soldier's Family. And we will also get half a pig and forty catties of New Year cakes."

"What crazy talk," Big Uncle said disgustedly. "Gone crazy thinking of pork and New Year cakes."

EARLY IN THE MORNING THE PIGS AND NEW ![13] Year cakes, carried in baskets dangling from flat-poles, were sent off to the Village Public Office. At home the house seemed empty and forlorn, like after a daughter's wedding when the guests have gone and all the hustle and bustle come to nothing. Moon Scent found that she could not settle down to her daily chores. She went next door to ask if Big Uncle had returned yet.

"He is not back yet," answered Big Aunt. And she leaned over to whisper, "I told him to smile nicely when they file in there with their flat-poles to hand over the presents. If you give ungraciously, you lose your things anyway, and get criticized on top of it."

"I hope Gold Root remembers to smile," Moon Scent said worriedly.

They chatted while waiting for the men to return.

"I hope he didn't pawn his wadded jacket and go off to gamble," said Moon Scent. "He's been feeling restless lately. Maybe I should go down to the teahouse and see if he is there."

"Don't go and look for him yourself. If you catch him there he'll feel embarrassed in front of all those people and there'll be another quarrel. Send Beckon."

Moon Scent shouted for Beckon and looked for her all over the place, but there was no trace of her.

"The little imp," said Moon Scent. "I saw her walking after her dad's load. Must have followed those rice cakes all the way to the temple!"

They were talking in the courtyard when Big Uncle scurried in excitedly.

"Close the door quick!" he said. "Bolt it quick! Come on—hurry! Where are the children? All at home? You people go inside at once!"

"What has happened?" asked Big Aunt.

Big Uncle finished bolting the door, then turned and whispered, "They are making a row."

"Who?"

"Where is Gold Root?" Moon Scent cut in.

"Don't mention Gold Root to me! This Gold Root with his temper! I always said one day he would get into serious trouble. Just now, when the New Year cakes were being weighed, Comrade Wong said that his contribution was underweight, so he started yelling. The others were also at fault—they all took it up. And they're all making a big row about it. Luckily I got away fast. Lost my flat-pole and baskets, though."

Moon Scent felt sick. "Big Uncle, have you seen Beckon?"

Big Uncle froze and then suddenly pointed a finger at her. "Hey, hurry up! Go and get her. Followed her pa all the way to the temple."

Then he complained fretfully of the necessity of unbolting the door now to let her out and then unbolting it again when she came back.

Moon Scent ran as fast as she could toward the temple. Her heart was curiously light and blank, an empty thing suspended in mid-air. From afar she could see the pink walls and hear the faint hubbub of shouting. She ran straight into the temple gate. The sun shone bright in the huge courtyard, which was quite empty. Sparrows twittered under the eaves. But suddenly a militiaman dashed out of the eastern wing with an arm outstretched, holding an archaic lance, the tuft of red hair under the blade fluffed out by the wind. It was a dreamlike, fantastic sight hauled down off the stage and thrust into the noonday sun. Moon Scent stood rooted to the spot while he charged past her and disappeared through the gate.

She padded up the stone steps and peered into the high-ceilinged gloom of the main hall. There was nobody to be seen. She turned and ran out of the temple. This time she could tell that the angry hum of the crowd came from the direction of Shen Ta Lumber Company, which had been requisitioned and was now the government storehouse. She rushed there, shouting, "Beckon! Beckon!"

The lumber company was a low building and once its name had been written in big black characters eight or nine feet high on the white wall. After the government took over the characters had been washed off, leaving big gray blotches. A dense crowd swarmed black against its door.

"Beckon, come home! Come home, Beckon's dad!" she cried.

Two militiamen brandishing red-tufted lances at the edge of the crowd also shouted, "Go home! All right, now—everybody go home!"

"We want to borrow some rice for the New Year!" someone called out.

"A good harvest and spend the New Year empty-bellied!"

"Not against the law—to borrow some rice!"

"What do you mean—'borrow'? It is our own grain!"

In the swift rise and fall of voices she could not tell which was her husband's. A strange excitement flooded over her that almost drowned out her anxiety and she was ashamed to call out, "Go home, Beckon's dad."

"Kinsmen," Comrade Wong's voice rose above the din, "whatever you have to say, we can talk it over. Whatever problems you have, we can settle it together. Everybody go home first and I guarantee——" The rest of his words were lost in the banging of carrying-poles against the door.

A child whimpered in fear and Moon Scent shrieked, "Beckon! Beckon!" as she pushed into the heart of the crowd.

"M-ma! M-ma!" yelled Beckon.

The militiamen began to thrust out tentatively with their lances and rods and someplace a man cried out in pain and swore, "Damn his mother! Somebody'll get killed!" as if surprised at the idea.

144

The carrying-poles continued to ram against the door. It creaked and then gave way with a crash.

"Kinsmen! Everybody keep cool. This is the People's Property! The People's Property cannot be touched!" Wong shouted hoarsely. "Let us all protect the People's Property!"

A carrying-pole struck him at the back of his head. Then the three militiamen who carried rifles pointed their guns at the crowd. One of the T'an brothers grabbed for one of the guns and the militiaman who held it shot him in the stomach. The other militiamen fired and the crowd was stunned into silence. Then the militiamen backed up, working the bolts of their rifles to reload, and the mob growled and surged toward them.

"Go up on the roof, you fools," yelled Wong, who had some experience in guerrilla warfare. "Shoot from the rooftop."

"M-ma! M-ma!" Beckon went on screaming flatly, with never the slightest variation in tone.

"Beckon! Beckon!" She was not far off but Moon Scent could not move an inch toward her, jammed tight in the stampede. In that nightmarish moment it was as if they had been calling to each other throughout eternity.

Comrade Wong grabbed Small Chang's gun from his terrified orderly and, holding the gun at his hip, fired blindly into the peasants pushing in past the shattered door. He reloaded rapidly and fired again. Desperately, he charged into the opening his shooting had created. Hands clutched at his clothes, but he swung the rifle back and forth and broke free. Badly bruised, his face

145

doubly pale with the blood on it, his clothes torn and his cap lost, he ran to his quarters in the western wing of the temple. Ku was in his room. He had been working on a "Glorious Family" poster when the riot broke out. Now he stood behind the table looking trapped.

"Where did they get the guns?" he quavered.

Wong made no reply as he slumped into a chair, his rifle across his knees and his chin embedded in the greasy, full bosom of his uniform.

"Are you hurt, Comrade?" Ku asked with belated solicitude.

"I'm all right," Wong answered dully.

"They have guns," Ku whispered.

"That was our militia defending the storehouse," Wong said stiffly.

"Oh," Ku said in some confusion.

The distant hubbub had died down but they could still hear scattered shots banging away. Wong drew the towel from the back of his waistband and wiped the sweat from his face and neck.

"We have failed," Wong said heavily, and then again, as if saying it for the first time, "We have failed. We have had to shoot at our people."

Ku avoided looking at him. In his present overwrought state Wong probably did not realize that this admission of failure in a moment of weakness and lack of faith amounted to a virtual betrayal of The Party and could be brought up against him in any purge. But sooner or later it would occur to him. And it would be only natural if he should want to dispose of the sole witness of his crime. Humble as his rank might be, within this village his power was absolute. And what was one more casualty amid all this shooting?

Wong stood up abruptly, and Ku jumped as the rifle in his lap fell clattering to the ground.

"There must be spies behind this," Wong said. He turned an excited, animated face and unseeing eyes toward Ku. "There must be. Otherwise the people would never rise up like this. We'll have to get to the bottom of this."

ON THEIR WAY TO TOWN TO REPORT TO THE **14**
district headquarters, the militiamen stopped
at Chou Village with a message for the *kan pu*. Then
the *kan pu* went round the village telling everybody to
t'i kao chin t'i, heighten their vigilance, and report at
once if they saw any suspicious characters around. A
number of *fan kê min*, anti-revolutionists, had escaped
and might have come in this direction.

That was all he said, but soon the word leaked out
that there had been a disturbance over at T'an Village.
Gold Flower felt concerned at the news. She wondered
what had happened and if any of her folks were affected.

At twilight she went out to fetch water. Balancing

the flat-pole on her shoulder, she walked absently down the flight of stone steps that led to the stream, her eyes fixed all the while on the opposite bank where her native village lay. With a slight tilt of one shoulder she lowered a pail into the stream and with a quiet twist of her body hoisted it back up again full. The darkening sky closed softly upon the darker hills and groves. Only the water was pale and bright, a broad band of shimmering gray.

A pebble hit her on the back.

"Little devil," she muttered without turning. In the village she was still referred to as The Bride, and children often followed her about, teasing her.

Another stone, glancing off her shoulder, fell splashing into the stream. The other pail filled, she slipped the pole off her shoulders and turned, hands on hips, to face the offender. There was nobody in sight.

"Sister! Sister Gold Flower!" someone called softly.

She jerked up her head. In no time she was up the slope, with the help of the flat-pole. In the bamboo grove she stood face to face with her sister-in-law, who looked like a ghost, clad only in a white shirt on top of her padded pants, with her hair disheveled and fuzzed out from her face.

"What's happened?" stammered Gold Flower.

When Moon Scent started to speak, her teeth chattered so much from the cold that she began to stammer, too, which annoyed her because it made her seem so frightened.

"Where is your padded jacket?" asked Gold Flower.

"Gold Root has it. He is weak from bleeding, so I made him put it over his shoulders."

"What's happened to him?" cried Gold Flower.

"He's all right," said Moon Scent, strangely defensive.

149

"They started shooting and he is hurt in the leg. It could have been much worse."

"Where is he now?"

"Farther up in the hill."

"Take me to see him."

Moon Scent hesitated. "You can't leave those pails down there. What if somebody comes and sees them?"

"But why did they shoot at him?" pressed Gold Flower.

"There was some trouble at the warehouse. People in the village wanted to borrow some rice for the New Year. And they started shooting." She added quickly, almost lightly, looking at Gold Flower with a bright expression, "Beckon is dead. Trampled to death."

"What?" Gold Flower said in an uncertain voice.

"We didn't believe it either. We took her with us all the way up the hill. But she is dead."

She told her about the shooting and how, as soon as she struggled free from the pressure of the stampeding mob, she had turned back toward the storehouse to look for Beckon. As she fought through the oncoming crowd, knocked off balance again and again, somebody seized her by the wrist and dragged her off in a fast run. It was Gold Root with Beckon slung over one shoulder. As they sped through the crackle of shots and bullets whining shrilly past them, she was conscious of her body as never before, feeling naked and vulnerable all over. But it could not be really serious, she felt, when they were running hand in hand like children in a game.

When he fell face downward she thought at first it was to take cover. Then, when she realized that he was wounded, she took Beckon's little body away from him and helped him up, making him lean on her. "We are almost home," she had said encouragingly.

"No, we are not going home," he had said. "We can't go home. We'll go somewhere else and hide for a few days; wait till the thing blows over."

She thought of going to her mother's place but that was too far, he wouldn't be able to make it. So they decided on Chou Village. They took a short cut through the hills because there was less chance of being seen.

It was one of those cold, sunless afternoons when the trees on the hill stood straight with their long white toes set wide apart on the ground, as if they were about to step down the hillside and walk right into the village, because it was too dreary up there. The hills rose in tiers, like steps cut out for their use. Moon Scent labored over those steps that were too high for men, dragging Gold Root after her. She had known for a long time that the limp, crushed child in her arms was dead. In the end, sheer exhaustion forced her to abandon her and there was no time for grief. They hid the small corpse at the base of one of the trees, hoping that no one would find it until they were farther away.

It was not till the end of the journey, when they had to cross the bridge, that she was truly afraid. It was nearing twilight. The narrow footbridge stood on high stilts black against the silvery pallor of the stream. In winter, when the water was low, the wobbly stilts rose to about thirty feet above water. Somehow she maneuvered Gold Root's unpredictably lurching weight across the twin line of long boards that felt soft and yielding under the feet. It felt awful to be cushioned all round with the infinite softness of empty air. And the broad expanse of water underneath was pale and withdrawn, falling far away from them.

She was glad now to have somebody to tell it to, all

151

the extraordinary things that happened during the day. But when she had finished her story, she could see that Gold Flower did not really understand, in spite of the dutifully assumed expression of shock and indignation on her face. The experience stood between them like a wall. They looked dumbly into each other's gray faces in the growing darkness, with the icy breath of the whispering bamboos blowing down their necks.

"So it's you people they are after," Gold Flower said in sudden realization. Her voice dropped to a whisper. "They said *fan kê-min*."

"*Fan kê-min!*" exclaimed Moon Scent. "How can we be *fan kê-min*?" But even as she protested she began to feel uncertain about the meaning of "reactionary," which had not been clear to her to begin with.

"We'll have to go away from here. We'll go to Shanghai. In Shanghai we can hide," she said with a note of finality. "But not just now—he can't even walk. He'll have to stay in your house for a few days."

Gold Flower's front teeth glistened faintly between parted lips in the dark. With an effort she closed her mouth to swallow. "But where can we hide him? My sisters-in-law and their children, they are all over the place."

"There must be some way to keep them out of your room."

"Not the children. They're running in and out all the time."

Moon Scent became silent, but not for long. "I know," she said. "You can say you've had a miscarriage and they will say your room is unclean and they won't come near it for months. And depend on them, they'll keep the children away."

"But they know I'm not pregnant."

"You were too shy to tell anybody," said Moon Scent.

Gold Flower could see that it was a workable scheme. There seemed to be no way out. This terrible thing that had happened was now intruding on her everyday world. She had duties there. She took it seriously, her new status as wife and daughter-in-law. She had to be careful with everything she did, or she would not be able to hold up her head in front of the ever-watchful enemies who were her sisters-in-law. She had left childhood far behind. And so had her brother, judging from the way he behaved that day when she came home to borrow money. He had outgrown his attachment to her.

She thought of many things as she slid a hand heavily up and down the long green arm of a bamboo. All she felt was its cold, smooth length and the knots that were loop bracelets on the arm.

"Sister Gold Flower," Moon Scent said gently, reaching for her hand, "I know it's hard for you. But your brother will die of cold if he stays outdoors all night. He'll die."

"But don't you see, it's dangerous for him to come into the village," said Gold Flower, flushed and resentful. "There's sure to be watchers."

"It's dark now. He'll lean on you and you can pretend it's Brother-in-Law coming home drunk."

Gold Flower stiffened at the mention of her husband. "No use saying it's him," she said in a hard voice. "He's been home all day. Everybody knows."

"Get him to come and fetch your brother then. Yes, it's better that he comes instead of you. The dogs know him well and they won't bark so much. Tell him to bring a padded blanket. Cover up your brother from head to

153

foot and say it's you. He has just fished you out of the stream. You have jumped in because you heard your family were all killed in the riot."

Gold Flower just stared at her dismally, not saying anything.

"Yes, that's much better," Moon Scent said upon reflection. "Nobody will fiddle with the blanket when it's supposed to be a young woman inside. Otherwise, they might want to have a look."

There was a short silence before Gold Flower said, "No, it won't do. He is sure to tell his mother."

"No, you mustn't let him tell anybody."

"I can't stop him. He'll be afraid. They will take him for a *fan kê-min*, if he is caught," she said miserably.

Moon Scent gave her a little push and whispered, "You talk to him, foolish girl. Talk to him nicely. A bride of two months, you can make him do anything."

"Foolish girl," indeed, Gold Flower thought bitterly. Her sister-in-law certainly took her to be a fool, to make her do this to her own husband—virtually luring him to his death. Did Moon Scent realize at all what she was asking of her? Perhaps she did not know what it was like to love one's husband. That Moon Scent had always been a hard and calculating woman.

Her brother himself would never have asked her to do a thing like that. He would understand. The memory of how good he had been to her suddenly flooded over her. And she remembered all that they had meant to each other throughout the years. She felt desolate, as if they were again left with nobody to turn to except each other.

There was no helping it—she had to do all she could for him. She jerked her hand away from Moon Scent's grasp and quickly turned to go, saying, "You wait here."

Moon Scent came a step after her, then stopped. "Sister Gold Flower," she said nervously.

Gold Flower flushed with shame at the thought that Moon Scent must think she was running away. "Don't worry," she said without turning, "I won't be long."

"Remember to have Brother-in-Law bring a padded blanket," said Moon Scent. "Here, you forgot your flat-pole." She hurried after her, bending down the slope to pass her the flat-pole.

"I was only afraid for Brother," Gold Flower said in a low voice, not looking at her.

After she was gone Moon Scent retreated to an upper ledge where the brush was denser. She was not at all sure of Gold Flower. "Now he'll find out—he who is so fond of his sister," she thought bitterly. "He'll see that the old saying is right. 'A daughter married off is water poured off'—and she won't come back. She might come home weeping and complain about her in-laws. But in times like this she thinks first about her husband's family."

She wondered if they should have risked the dogs and sneaked into the village by themselves. Once Gold Root was inside the house, they would have more of a hold over the Chous. The Chous would realize that they were involved already and they would have to help keep the secret, out of fear.

She hugged herself tight in the icy wind. Myriads of tongue-like bamboo leaves were making that dry, eerie hush-hush noise that was the most chilling sound on earth. It was hard to stand still in this cold, but she was afraid to walk about or stamp her feet to keep warm.

Lights dotted the village. On the other side, the vast gray plain lay stretched out in the evening haze. Its silence was full of small, muffled rustlings like the sound of a man sniffing and turning inside a padded blanket, kept awake by the cold.

The first time Moon Scent ever came to this village was when the match was being made between Gold Flower and the Chou boy. The Chous had taken special notice of Gold Flower in the crowd during the annual parade of the gods. But the T'ans had never seen the boy and it was arranged that they should come to Chou Village one day while he was at work in the fields. They took Gold Flower along and urged her to have a good look, but she had perversely turned her head away when they passed the rice paddies. And yet later, during discussions, when somebody remarked on the boy's good looks, she had said scornfully, "Looks so sissy with the earrings." It was a standing joke in the family, how she could have seen without looking. The Chou boy's parents had been afraid to lose him as a baby, so they had had his ears pierced and made him wear silver earrings like a girl to deceive the jealous gods.

They had come to Chou Village that day on the pretext of going to town to sell their lamb and chickens at the fair. To increase its weight, the lamb had been stuffed with food before they set out. Its incredibly swollen belly, hard as a big ball of rock, hung low and swung with every step. But that did not stop it from prancing happily ahead of them. The chickens and ducks were in one basket dangling from the flat-pole on Gold Root's shoulder. The basket at the other end held Beckon, who was a baby then and could not be left alone at home. Leaning forward, with both hands holding on to the edge of the basket, she looked out at the world with her bright, fixed gaze.

156

Moon Scent sobbed at the recollection, trying to be as quiet as she could about it. The fit of weeping finally passed. She could tell by the night noises and the dwindling lights in the village that it was getting late. Her first uneasiness about Gold Flower had turned to fear.

It was now almost pitch dark. With a start she perceived a moving figure outlined against the shimmer of the water down below. From the little hard knot of hair at the back of the head she could tell a moment later that it was an elderly woman. With a sinking heart she realized it was Gold Flower's mother-in-law, coming in her direction without a lantern.

Gold Flower must have let out the secret, by accident or on purpose.

"The cheap slave girl!" Moon Scent swore under her breath. "The putrid, dead slave girl!"

She took some time to decide whether it would be wise to reveal herself.

There was a rustling in the blackness below. "Sister-in-Law Gold Root," the woman whispered. "Sister-in-Law Gold Root."

"*Ta-niung*, Aunt, save us," Moon Scent whispered back, materializing at her side.

"*Ai-yah*, Sister-in-Law Gold Root," the woman exclaimed warmly, groping for her hands. "A good thing I heard about this in time! You know Gold Flower is a mere child. And that son of mine—the two of them are just a pair of children. If you depended on them to help you it would be disastrous."

Moon Scent understood that she was being reprimanded for daring to go behind her back. "We were desperate, *Ta-niung*," she murmured. "We have nobody to turn to. I am so glad you came. I have always known you have a kind heart."

"Lucky I found out in time," the woman repeated, "or it would be all up with you. Our place is so small and crowded and there are many people in the family. 'A bottle's mouth can be stoppered. But not human mouths.'"

"Don't blame it on the others. You yourself would be the first to report us," thought Moon Scent.

"You know even ordinarily we have to report at once if a relative stays overnight. And now—you can imagine how dangerous it would be, when they have just been in to warn us. At the word *fan kê-min*, who is not afraid?"

"But we are nothing of the sort, *Ta-niung*—we haven't done anything."

She brushed aside Moon Scent's protests. "Yes, and they told us, 'If you know where they are and do not speak out, you are accomplices. And you'll be tied up with ropes and sent up to the district headquarters.' Why, it is worse than harboring runaway landlords!"

Again Moon Scent tried to explain but she would not listen. "Now that it has come to this, the only thing that can save you is to go to town and take the boat there. A good thing you are well-traveled and know the way to the city." She pushed a small bundle into Moon Scent's hand. "Here, I brought you some food. I must go now. I dare not stay long—it would be dangerous for you as well as for us."

Moon Scent clutched at her sleeves. "*Ta-niung*, I kneel to you." She sank to her knees sobbing, overcome by despair and her humiliation before this hateful woman.

"No, no, Sister-in-Law Gold Root, don't do that!" The

older woman tried to lift her to her feet and, failing that, also knelt down. By returning the obeisance she showed that she did not accept it and so was not put under an obligation by the other's humility. "Don't think I don't want to help you. It is all for your own good. Go—as fast as you can. It's not safe around here. All our neighbors have been alerted."

"He cannot walk, *Ta-niung*. Perhaps we can hide in the hills for a few days, if *Ta-niung* can tell Gold Flower to send us some food now and then."

The woman said sharply, "How can you spend the night outdoors in this freezing weather? And at daytime you might be seen by woodcutters."

"We can go higher up in the hills."

"Higher up there are wolves." She heaved herself to her feet with difficulty, trying to wrench herself free of Moon Scent's hand. "No use your pestering me. Start to town right now, while it is dark."

Moon Scent sobbed aloud, hanging on to the woman's clothes. "How can we go to town with him bleeding like this? How can we get past the sentry at the boat landing?"

"Better go while you can, Sister-in-Law Gold Root," the woman said meaningfully. "I did not want to tell you this, but—go quickly. I am not sure that one of my sons hasn't already reported you."

She broke away, and was gone.

Moon Scent believed her last words were merely a threat to hurry them along. However, one never knew.

She labored uphill, hugging the parcel of foodstuff close to her body as if it warmed her. And the thought that she was a bringer of food as well as bad news was a ray of warmth in the midst of her desolation. Everything looked different in the dark. She had difficulty finding that place where she had left Gold Root propped up against a tree. At first she thought it was that tall tree over there but she must have been mistaken. The way always seemed longer when it was unfamiliar, she reminded herself, especially in a hostile country where every step was dangerous.

But as she walked on the feeling grew on her that she had already passed the spot. With mounting panic she turned back to explore the region more carefully. Where was he? She had been a long time. Had they got him? Or—and she clutched at this idea—had he seen or heard something that frightened him and had hidden himself somewhere?

"Where are you?" she whispered, groping around. "Beckon's dad, where are you?"

The open spaces closed around her. Her throat, swollen from so much whispering, hurt as if it had a thick iron ring clamped on it.

Wolves! The smell of blood must have lured them down the hill. As a rule they never ventured as far down as this but they might, in times like this. Quite irrationally she assumed that the wolves, like human beings, were suffering from the man-made famine.

But then she reasoned with a horrible practicality that if it was the wolves they would have left something, shoes, or a hand. They were not so neat in their habits. She searched everywhere in the vicinity. Then she found herself looking down at a tree on the bank of the stream. There was something odd about that small tree outlined against the gray pallor of the water. What seemed to be a large bird's nest nestling in its forked branches was too big, and far too low.

She scrambled down the slope. With numb, icy hands she reached for the bundle on the tree. It was his padded jacket with the sleeves tied together to make a neat bundle. Wrapped carefully inside was her padded jacket. In a moment she understood as well as if he had spoken to her.

The pale, luminous stream washed past at her feet. He had taken with him his padded pants which were torn and bloodstained and past saving. But his jacket, though old, was still serviceable, so he left it to her.

He wanted her to have a fair chance of getting away. He must have known that his wound was more serious than she was willing to admit. He never said anything about it. But now that she thought back, just before she left him under that tree, when she straightened up after seeing that he was comfortably settled, she had felt his fingers close around her ankle with what seemed then to be a childish impulsiveness, and he had held on to her as if he did not want her to go. She realized now that that was his moment of indecision. The feel of his fingers around her ankle was so real and solid, the moment was so close at hand and yet forever out of reach, it drove her nearly frantic.

After a long time she finally bestirred herself, put on her jacket and buttoned it up. His jacket she wrapped around her loosely with the sleeves tied under her chin. Gone thin and hard with wear, the padded jacket stood up stiffly about her ears. She rubbed her face on it.

Slowly at first, then with quickened pace, she set out for home.

AT BIG UNCLE'S THEY DID NOT EVEN DARE **15**
light the lamp that night. They spoke in
whispers, though Big Uncle always coughed loudly
when he shuffled about, for fear that he would bump
against his daughter-in-law and make himself a figure of
ridicule.

"Did I not always say so: one day these people would
get into big trouble," he muttered.

Big Aunt scolded her daughter-in-law in a low voice.
"Whispering to Gold Root's wife all day long, rushing
over there whenever people were not looking. Now this
is fine! Maybe they'll also come and get you. And once

they say 'anti-revolutionist' do you still expect to live? You think they say it just for fun?"

Sister-in-Law Gold Have Got wept with fright.

"Since they came here to search the house, it must be that those two were still alive and in hiding somewhere," Big Uncle speculated matter-of-factly. "Might have escaped to town and taken the boat from there."

"How can they get on a boat without a pass? Didn't you hear what she said when she came back? How many questions they ask at the boat landing!"

The militiamen came again during the evening. Peeping through the window in the darkened house, the old couple saw them enter bearing lanterns. They came out again carrying off Ku's luggage on a flat-pole. It must be that Ku was staying with Comrade Wong for the night, for safety's sake.

The militiamen neglected to latch tight the door to Gold Root's rooms. It slammed all night in the wind so that Big Aunt could not sleep, and she called out to her daughter-in-law to get up and shut it tight.

"*Ae*, we must not touch it—must not touch it," Big Uncle said in alarm. "If people find out about it, they might think we took something from those rooms. Then when all their things are confiscated, the blame will be put on us if anything is missing."

The door banged on with shattering savagery.

Big Aunt lay awake for a long time listening to it. Then she whispered to her husband, "I do not think it is the wind. It sounds like those two coming back."

"Don't talk nonsense!" said Big Uncle, who was thinking the same.

Then Big Aunt realized with a shock that she had spoken of those two as if they were already ghosts. They might still be alive and it would bring them bad luck like a curse. In her contrition she thought of all their goodness, and their youth. And her tears fell onto her hard, flat old pillow of blue cloth stuffed with the white plumes of reeds.

WONG'S QUARTERS IN THE TEMPLE WAS A **16** dreary place but to Ku, after staying with the peasants, its aura of literacy made it almost like home. The room was long and enormous, formerly the chamber of some minor god. The shrines and idols had been cleared away but not the age-old dust and cobwebs. An oil lamp lit up the only furnished corner, where a bed and a littered table and some chairs and benches made up the combined sleeping quarters and office. This small area was pervaded by an odor that country people call "the old widower's smell," caused by loneliness, dirt, and general neglect. It hung all the more heavily in the intense cold of the night.

Ku sat on the bed nervously plucking hairs off his upper lip. Outside in the great hall of the temple they were torturing the men arrested for the riot.

"*Ai-yah! Ai-yaw!*" came the rhythmic groans. "*Uh-ee-ee-yah!*" The voice would weaken and trail off, then suddently turn into a straight, bestial howl, tremendously strong.

This could not be true, Ku thought. It was like a traveler in one of those ghost stories taking shelter in the porches of a temple at night and being wakened by the sound of the gods holding court over the dead. Peeping at the brightly lit scene, the man in the story recognized a dead relative undergoing cruel tortures. He screamed. And everything went black and all was quiet in the temple.

Scream, and perhaps it would all vanish. In the city it had always been asserted that the Communists never used torture. All the stories of the torture of landlords and suspected spies were lies spread by enemy agents.

But what he found hardest to take was that these men groaning on the "tiger stool" were plain farmers. He knew that Wong knew they could not be tools of spies and saboteurs, as he had told the village. Of course it would sound better in a report to put it that way and would save face for Wong. But if he was that unscrupulous, Ku had better start to worry for his own life.

"Don't imagine things," he said to himself. He had a desperate need to believe in Wong and what he stood for. For the thousandth time since the Communists came, Ku told himself, "Believe—for your own good." It had become like opium for the intellectuals, this faith which would enable them to suffer privations cheerfully, deaden all disquieting thoughts and feelings, still the conscience, and generally make life bearable.

He was facing a severe test, Ku told himself. He would have to overcome his petty-bourgeois Tender Emotionalism. Of course this riot of hungry peasants was a mere accident, an isolated instance which had no place in the general picture. Represented in all its distressing aspects, it would be detrimental to government prestige and would, in the long run, work against the good of The People. Therefore it was important to show The People that it was an incident engineered by enemy agents. Wong had to be thorough about it. He had to get some kind of story out of the rioters, hammer it into shape and see that they all said more or less the same thing by the time they were delivered to the district headquarters.

But he found it hard to reason along such lines when he thought of Moon Scent. He could not help feeling concerned over her fate. If she had been captured and was crying out right now under torture, he doubted that he could keep his head.

A door creaked open in the far end of the room, beyond the reach of the lamplight. Ku looked up, half-expecting to see Moon Scent entering with his nightly warming basket which was at once his comfort and his shame.

It was Comrade Small Chang, the militiaman, coming to get some cigarettes for Comrade Wong. He looked for them under Wong's pillow.

"It looks like nobody is going to get any sleep tonight," he complained, yawning. "Comrade Wong works too hard."

"Yes, he really should rest," Ku said, smiling politely. "Especially when he's been hurt."

"He really should have some rest. Just have them hung upside down for the night. Tomorrow they'd talk, all right."

Ku inquired casually if Gold Root T'an and his wife had been caught yet. Small Chang replied that he had not heard anything about it.

It must have been very late when Wong turned in. Half-asleep, Ku was aware of the boards creaking on the bed and the sound of spitting. The light went out. Then the snoring woke him up completely. The man sounded as if he was drinking—gulping down the dense black night in huge draughts, pausing now and then to let out a small, contented sigh.

Ku did not realize it, but he must have managed to drift off to sleep again, for he woke up with a start. A deafening volley of shots still clattered in the hills. The next thing he knew, Comrade Small Chang was in the room, an oil lamp in his hand.

"The storehouse is on fire, Comrade Wong!" shouted Small Chang.

Struggling into his padded uniform, Wong barked, "Blow out that lamp!"

But Small Chang, not having had any combat experience, could see no sense in the order and did not know whether he had heard aright. In the confusion Ku remembered seeing Wong's sleep-swollen face under his bandaged forehead; it had an orange glow in the flickering lamplight. And he thought he saw a gleam in Wong's eyes that was almost like joy. It must have eased his conscience—the realization that it was actually the Nationalist underground who were at the back of all this.

For some reason the firing had ceased by the time Wong rushed outdoors. But dogs were barking, while militiamen ran beating gongs wildly from one end of the village to the other, giving the fire alarm. Off in the distance they could hear shouts of "Fire! Help stop the fire!"

Wong, with his bandaged head, was rushing to and fro shouting himself hoarse. "Kinsmen! Everybody help stop the fire! Save the storehouse! It's the People's Grain!"

But the crowd hung back, mindful of the gunfire a while ago, until somebody suddenly exclaimed, "Why, that was the firecrackers in the storehouse! Firecrackers set off by the fire!"

The word was spread around, and when it reached Ku inside the temple he took heart and ventured outdoors to do his share of fire fighting.

People scurried from all sides toward the stream with buckets and containers of all sorts. Some worked doggedly. They loved with an impersonal, unthinking affection the rice that was the fruit of their labor, and their hearts ached more than any miser's to see the great hoard going up in flames. Others were gleeful at this unforeseen turn of events which avenged their own people killed in the riot. However, they put up a creditable display of enthusiasm, yelling at others to "stop the fire," dashing down the banks for water, only to spill most of it on the way.

The spilt water froze instantly, making the ground very slippery. Ku was splashing along with a brimming bucket when he slipped and fell, emptying the icy water over himself with the staggering impact of a blow. His chin dug into the cloth-covered surface of a padded hardness which for a sharp, frightful instant he took for his own leg. Then to his horror he discovered that he had fallen over one of the corpses left lying in this vicinity. His hands flew to the glasses on his face, feeling for them and straightening them as he scrambled to his feet. They might well have been broken. And it was this last awful thought that demoralized him completely. He retired from the scene to become the sole onlooker, shivering as the water soaked through his jacket.

They were still beating away at the gongs. The ceaseless clanging awakened an ancient terror, as if the village was being invaded by bandits. Across the grounds bathed in the wild crimson glow militiamen dashed away brandishing their red-tufted lances. One of them claimed he had seen a woman sneaking away when the blaze first started and he had chased her right into the fire.

As he watched, the gongs and the soaring flames roused a wild, primitive exultation in Ku. "But this is just what I am looking for," he thought. "A splendid and stirring spectacle for the climax of my film. Just move the story a few years back. Recount how the peasants under the old regime were driven by hunger to rob and burn the storehouse."

Then he remembered that there had been explicit instructions in the leading magazines for literary people. Writers were not to dwell on the unsavory past as if with a lingering relish, but to turn to the bright, new, constructive side. "Rather than curse the darkness, praise the light!"

He cursed anyway, watching the dying fire. The storehouse had been picked clean to the bones. The frame stood out clear in the brilliant sheet of flames. Giant black cinders perched birdlike on the beams. Aptly called "fire magpies and fire crows," those evil birds sat in a row, turning their heads this way and that with dreadful tranquillity in the softening golden light.

"WAIT A MOMENT," GOLD FLOWER SAID TO **17**
her husband Plenty Own as they were walking away from the *Hsien* Public Security Bureau. The
strap on one of her cloth shoes had come loose. To button
it up she stood on one foot, putting a hand on his arm to
steady herself.

Gold Flower had been summoned to the market town
to identify a corpse found in the river. It could have
drifted there from upstream and the description fitted
Gold Root, but they wanted her confirmation.

It had been a hard day for her, Plenty Own told himself. The long walk along the river to the market town
and the farmers they passed staring at the two of them

walking between the policemen. Then the view of the body, stretched out on a rough trestle under the light of a single electric lamp in the shed in back of the police station. Aware of the police eyes watching them for some sign of emotion, Plenty Own stared down at the corpse of his brother-in-law, mildly surprised that he had no more feeling than he did. "My brother," he heard his wife say quietly.

It was the first time he had seen a bullet hole; the wound in the flesh of the thigh had been washed clean and the lips of the hole were almost bloodless. The police led them outside for questioning. Finally a comrade in charge was satisfied, asked them to sign some papers they could not read, and let them go. The final question of the disposal of the body—"We'll take care of things unless you have some other plan," the comrade had said meaningly. Plenty Own nodded; it would be better if they didn't bring Gold Root back to their own village.

While Gold Flower was leaning on him to button her shoe he brought his face close to hers with a slight turn of his head. He was not looking at her, but she felt self-conscious at this expression of sympathy and her face became more set in its absorbed, inward look that masked her feelings, or rather the absence of them.

Any shock she might have felt at the sight of her brother's body had been well insulated by the numbing sense of strangeness all round. Above all, it was strange to be walking about with her husband in town in the evening. They seldom ever went out together. Just now, in their long trip to town, they had been oppressed by the ominous presence of the two policemen who accompanied them, but now they were by themselves. Plenty Own took care not to betray the pleasure he felt. He would have been very surprised to learn that it was shared.

They came to the wharf with all the lighted boats bobbing below in the shimmering darkness. In the dim gold interior of one sampan they could see a bamboo tube nailed on the wall of matting to hold a bunch of red-lacquered chopsticks. On other craft the oil lamps shone through the wash lines. One boat was dark; on the stern a silhouetted figure stood urinating into the river.

Coolies carrying goods and luggages on bamboo poles side-stepped cautiously down the dizzy gray flight of broad, shallow stone steps, a huge, ancient pile of stones dreamlike under the yellow electric light. Rifled militiamen shouted questions across the water. Owners of boats who had a touch of the gangster about them swaggered down the steps with their padded jackets unbuttoned down the front and their leather slippers flip-flapping loudly.

Past the wharf the water front became dark and deserted. The shops were still closed for the New Year. But farther down there seemed to be something going on and a small crowd had collected around it. Gold Flower and her husband stopped to look. A bystander explained, "It's that boatman who got drunk on New Year's Eve and fell overboard. A strange time to die—on New Year's Eve. So they're holding the ceremony here on the riverbank."

About seven or eight mourners knelt in a row, each holding the one in front of him by the waist. The head mourner who knelt in front was a little boy, probably the son of the drowned man. The traditional white cloth curtain wound around the mourners, ending in a knot tied over the boy's forehead. The weeping must have been going on for a long time. The men were hoarse and the women merely moaned weakly, with much murmuring under their breaths. But there was one of them who set up a weird, high-pitched howl that went over their heads, on and off, like a doleful wind. The boy's head dipped forward rhythmically with the fits of weeping, bowing lower and lower. Set before him on the ground was a basket of ashes holding joss sticks.

There were more joss sticks and a tall white pair of lighted candles on a square table that stood a little way off. Two men who were neither monks nor Taoist priests sat side by side at the head of the table. These were professional reciters of popular Buddhist verses. They were both about thirty, looking like shop assistants in their shabby long gowns. They intoned the verses in unison, their bodies swaying from side to side in the manner of schoolboys reading out loud. The long, rambling half-prayer was in Chinese instead of Sanskrit but Gold Flower could make out only a few lines here and there. It mentioned the name of the deceased and the place he had come from, the age he had attained, the surname of his wife's family, the number and sex of his children. It spoke of all this with a quiet satisfaction and prayed for his speedy passage into another existence as a human being, preferably a man.

"I'll have the same rites performed for Brother," Gold Flower suddenly said to herself. "Not right now, but later when this talk of *fan kê-min* has blown over." She felt it would free him from the painfully extraordinary circumstances of his death and make him the same as everybody else. The prayer seemed to have this effect. While the voices droned on by the flickering candlelight on the darkening shore, the dead man was being gently lowered into the sea of humanity.

She promised her brother's spirit then and there that she would arrange for the recitation of prayers and also the adoption of a boy child for his heir, that he might be mourned properly. She would bring up the child and later see to his marriage so that her brother's branch of the family would not die out. She would do her duty toward the T'ans as she had toward the Chous. Her eyes brimmed with tears at the thought of all that she would do for her brother. And she truly grieved for him for the first time since disaster befell him.

The child to be adopted had to be born a T'an. Perhaps Big Aunt might be persuaded to part with one of her grandsons. She had several.

It had been snowing. Big Aunt went out into the fields early in the morning, carrying her warming basket with her, with live charcoal buried in the ashes inside. There was a teen-aged militiaman posted at the village gate which was being watched night and day—the tension was not yet over. The boy whispered to her banteringly, seeing the basket, "Going to set fire to the storehouse again, Big Aunt?"

"Don't talk nonsense." Big Aunt looked nervously around her. "My grandson is so terribly sick, and you have the heart to joke with me."

It was her youngest grandson. Everybody said he must have "run against something," crossed the path of some spirit and incurred its displeasure. It was hardly surprising, seeing that there had been so many deaths in the village.

Big Aunt knew exactly what it was.

The day after the fire, when the villagers had been set to work clearing up the rubble, a body had been discovered in a cave made between two walls propped up by each other when they had caved in. It was in a sitting position and was a smooth, bright pinkish red all over. The color had stood out glaringly against the charred ruins. It had occurred to Big Aunt—to all of them, in fact, who had been there—that the seated figure suggested one of the bald, slim images of Arhans lined up on both sides of a temple. She had been deeply shocked and awed. She also remembered that monks when they die are always cremated in a big jar, sitting up. It was very odd and would seem to speak of divine origins in Gold Root's wife—for the body was that of a woman and she knew that it was she. This Moon Scent must have been at least a gifted monk in her last life.

She had known it was Moon Scent, but, like everybody else, she had held her tongue. It was one thing to take part in the riot and another thing to burn down the storehouse. Even if it had been generally suspected that it was one of themselves who had done it, it was best to leave matters vague. Who would know in what form retribution would come? The whole village might be demolished as in the Japanese days.

Even the Chairman of the Farmers' Association had pretended that he could not tell who it was. Then Comrade Wong had appeared on the scene and insisted that it was Moon Scent. And the militiaman on duty at the storehouse the night before had turned up and excitedly repeated his story of having chased a prowler back into the burning building.

"I wouldn't be surprised if it was Gold Root T'an's wife," the Chairman of the Farmers' Association had finally admitted. "She's been away for three years working in the city. Who knows what bad company she might have got into, spies and Kuomingtang agents? Here she's been back scarcely a month and this has happened. Must have been sent here on a special mission."

Then Big Aunt had chimed in, "I'm not one to speak ill of the dead, but that one is a real fox and a broom-star.[1] I've always known that she couldn't be trusted alone in the city. Must have picked up some gangster, some *fan kê-min*. Poor Gold Root—she led him around by the nose. See how he had changed after she came back, and he used to be so good and progressive. Ask Comrade Wong. And the way she beat her little girl! Just like a stepmother! Ask Comrade Ku. He knows. And the things she said to me when we had our quarrel! I never spoke a single word to her after that. Never. Ask anybody."

Afterward, when she had returned home, she had found that her grandson was down with fever. She hadn't said anything to Sister-in-Law Gold Have Got, not wishing to alarm her. But in her heart she had quickly addressed herself to Moon Scent, "Now don't be angry, Sister-in-Law Gold Root. 'When alive you were human; after death you are divine.' You won't stoop to plague a child, will you? And when he's your nephew, too."

The child's fever had mounted during the night. This morning Big Aunt had gone out grimly resolved to burn joss money at Moon Scent's grave and risk being caught at it.

"He's your nephew, remember," she kept murmuring to Moon Scent. "I might have offended you but his mother hasn't. You used to be such good friends, remem-

[1] A broom-star is a meteor which is regarded as a bringer of ill-luck and has come to stand for a woman who ruins her husband.

ber? Spare the boy, and when he grows up he'll burn joss money at your grave at the New Year and all the important festivals. He'll be like a son to you."

The snow-laden bamboos by the roadside had thick, fat white leaves. The green undersides of the leaves wove in and out of the whiteness when the wind came. The ashes in her basket got blown into her face. She would light the joss money with the live charcoal. Her eyes and nose were running in the stinging cold. The arm was getting cramped that held the long string of silver paper cups under her padded jacket. It had to be held high so that it would not show, and slightly away from the body so as not to crush the flimsy silver paper.

The chirp of hungry birds sounded surprisingly loud in the silence of the padded universe. Her eyes scanned the fields for Moon Scent's grave, which she knew would be difficult to locate. The body had been rolled up in a mat and laid in a shallow hole which was merely covered up, with no mound built above it.

She saw a yellow patch way over there beside the forked footpath. "Is that it?" she wondered. "That couldn't be the earth showing through the snow, could it? No snow on her grave!" Her knees went weak with awe.

The sound of dogs snarling floated across the distance, faint but with a distilled clearness. She wiped her eyes and saw that the heaving yellow patch was a pack of wild dogs fighting over the grave. They must have burrowed into the ground and pawed it open. She thought she could see a corner of the straw mat showing under the heaped canine bodies.

"It's a sin. It's a sin," Big Aunt muttered as she moved away, flooded with relief. "She certainly can't do anybody any harm," she thought, "if she can't even protect her own bones."

Ku had been sitting facing Comrade Wong every day across the desk. Wong with his graying bandages had many reports to write and Ku busied himself with his script. He had finally managed to work the fire into his story of the dam. No small problem, because how can a dam burn?

The way the story went now, the engineer and old peasants collaborated to solve the problem of the annual floods by building a dam across the stream. However, in this village lived a landlord who had survived the Land Reform through the generosity of the government. He was allowed his acre of land like everybody else and so far he still managed to live better than the others, with much furtive feasting and hasty clearing of dishes when the authorities called. And the potbellied old man still enjoyed the company of a beautiful girl, presumably his concubine. Perhaps it would be better not to stress her marital status since concubinage should not continue to exist under the People's Government. Her main function was to lean decoratively against the table by the light of the flickering lamp and lend atmosphere to the various treasonable dealings of the dispossessed landlord. She would look something like Moon Scent. Ku had refrained from going down to see the body found in the storehouse after the fire, so his memory of her remained unspoiled. In the film it would be summer and the girl would be wearing a striped cotton summer shirt. It would have to be decorously sacklike, but stripes could do wonders.

The landlord was approached by a spy who enlisted his services, conferring on him the rank of a general in the Nationalist Army. Accompanied by his concubine, the landlord skulked out at night to bomb the new dam. A vigilant militiaman detected them in time but they managed to get away without being identified.

When the spy put pressure on him to show some results, the landlord in desperation set fire to the government storehouse. He was caught red-handed, together with the concubine who scurried in his wake, carrying a small bundle. They were probably thinking of fleeing the country after the deed. The bundle contained, among other valuables, his treasured credentials of a Nationalist general.

Ku was well pleased with the story. It was a neat piece of work. But it would have to be a very small fire. One or two sacks of rice had barely started to smoke when a guard had already rounded the corner shouting, "Fire! Fire! Saboteurs!" Otherwise it would reflect on the efficiency of the local militia. Wrathful newspapers would call it "the indiscriminate use of the weapon of satire on the people's own organizations . . . far exceeding the bounds of constructive criticism." The film would not be banned, which would attract too much attention to it, but just quietly withdrawn in the middle of its showing. And any chance of making a name for himself would be gone for good.

The comfort visit to the Soldiers' Families had to be postponed because the firecrackers had been destroyed in the fire and at this late date it was impossible to replace them. After the fifth day of the first moon, when the shops reopened after the New Year, Comrade Wong got up another collection from the farmers and made a special trip to town to buy more firecrackers.

Early next morning the people assembled outside the Village Public Office. The paraders lined up. The Rice-Sprout Song Corps went in front; after them came the gift bearers. They struck up the gongs and cymbals. The dancers started the routine steps, the men and women side by side in two rows, their painted cheeks startlingly red in the cold gray morning light. The gift bearers crouched under their flat-poles and then straightened up with an effort. The pale, bloated halves of slaughtered pigs, cut lengthwise, dangled at the ends of the poles. Pigs' heads sitting in trays had little pink paper flowers tucked rakishly in their ears. Other trays held the white slabs of New Year cakes, hard as bricks, stacked into high mounds.

Comrade Wong saw that the two lines of dancers were straggly from the loss of men in the riot. He motioned to Comrade Small Chang, who went up to the elderly folks standing around looking, and spoke to them. Presently the old men and women, smiling helplessly and pushing each other along, sidled up to the dancers. Big Uncle and Big Aunt were among them. Their old faces puckered in their habitual half-frown, half-smile, they tried to "wriggle the Rice-Sprout Song," throwing their arms creakily back and forth.

Comrade Wong turned to find Ku standing by his side. He jerked his head toward Big Aunt as she danced past. "Sixty-seven this year," he said, smiling, "and so enthusiastic."

"Sixty-eight with the New Year," Big Aunt corrected him jauntily, as if slightly offended.

"Sixty-eight," Wong repeated to Ku with pride.

The dancing stopped soon after they passed into the open fields, to be resumed later when they drew near the neighboring village. But the gift bearers kept up their mincing gait in co-ordination with the bouncing carcasses of pigs hanging from their flat-poles. They proceeded slowly along the winding footpath that led across the tawny brown plain. The gongs and cymbals went on beating loudly,

"CHONG, CHONG! CHI CHONG CHI!
CHONG, CHONG! CHI CHONG CHI!"

But under the immense open sky the sound was muffled and strangely faint.

Eileen Chang, 1961
Courtesy of Crown Publishing Company, Ltd., Taipei, Taiwan.